The harvest

Hannah realized that in coming directly from the village, without so much as a moment to collect her thoughts, she had paused at her rush hut only long enough to snatch the Wizard's cup from its shelf, not steep the tea to fill it. Incredulity swept over her, and shame.

She managed only to stammer, "I forgot!"

The Wizard's eyes narrowed, gaze combing through her locks.

"Ah," he muttered, nodding to himself. "Now I see what's caused your wildness." One hand darted like a hawk's pounce to her hair. He grasped her firmly by the arm. "We must have them out!"

His clasp was adamant, his fingers forcible. She could not have escaped him had she tried. Her ears rang, temples pounding as every shoot and stalk, blossom and twig rooted among her tresses was zealously seized and wrested, sometimes by twos and threes. She had to bite her lip to keep from screaming. . . .

FIREBIRD
WHERE FANTASY TAKES FLIGHT™

The Beggar Queen   Lloyd Alexander

The Changeling Sea   Patricia A. McKillip

Crown Duel   Sherwood Smith

The Dreaming Place   Charles de Lint

The Ear, the Eye and the Arm   Nancy Farmer

Enchantress from the Stars   Sylvia Engdahl

Fire Bringer   David Clement-Davies

Growing Wings   Laurel Winter

The Hex Witch of Seldom   Nancy Springer

The Kestrel   Lloyd Alexander

I Am Mordred   Nancy Springer

I Am Morgan Le Fay   Nancy Springer

Mariel of Redwall   Brian Jacques

Mattimeo   Brian Jacques

Mossflower   Brian Jacques

The Outlaws of Sherwood   Robin McKinley

Redwall   Brian Jacques

The Riddle of the Wren   Charles de Lint

Spindle's End   Robin McKinley

Westmark   Lloyd Alexander

The Winter Prince   Elizabeth E. Wein

Treasure at the Heart of the Tanglewood

by

Meredith Ann Pierce

FIREBIRD

AN IMPRINT OF PENGUIN PUTNAM INC.

FIREBIRD
Published by the Penguin Group
Penguin Putnam Inc.,
345 Hudson Street, New York, New York 10014, U.S.A.
Penguin Books Ltd, 80 Strand, London WC2R ORL England
Penguin Books Australia Ltd,
250 Camberwell Road, Camberwell, Victoria 3124, Australia
Penguin Books Canada Ltd, 10 Alcorn Avenue, Toronto, Ontario, Canada M4V 3B2
Penguin Books (N.Z.) Ltd, 182-190 Wairau Road, Auckland 10, New Zealand

Penguin Books Ltd, Registered Offices: Harmondsworth, Middlesex, England

First published in the United States of America by Viking,
a division of Penguin Putnam Books for Young Readers, 2001
Published by Firebird, an imprint of Penguin Putnam Inc., 2003

1 3 5 7 9 10 8 6 4 2

THE LIBRARY OF CONGRESS HAS CATALOGED THE VIKING EDITION AS FOLLOWS:

Pierce, Meredith Ann.
Treasure at the heart of the Tanglewood / Meredith Ann Pierce
p. cm.
Summary: Hannah, a healer with unusual powers, leaves the wizard she
has always served and, along with her animal companions, begins
a journey which uncovers the truth about her real nature.
ISBN 0-670-89247-3
[1. Identity—Fiction. 2. Wizards—Fiction. 3. Magic—Fiction. 4. Fantasy.]
I. Title. PZ7.P61453 Tr 2001 [Fic]—dc21 00-51366

ISBN 0-14-250013-5

Printed in the United States of America

For TPG, MPG, and FKG,

my very own treasures

at the heart of the tanglewood.

—MAP

Table of Contents

Chapter 1	Brown Hannah	1
Chapter 2	Wizard	12
Chapter 3	Rumors	23
Chapter 4	Village	32
Chapter 5	Tanglewood's Crux	42
Chapter 6	Lies	50
Chapter 7	Mending	58
Chapter 8	Black Knight	68
Chapter 9	Foxkith	80
Chapter 10	Lovestruck	90
Chapter 11	Golden Boar	99
Chapter 12	Thorns	108

Chapter 13	Green Hannah	117
Chapter 14	Needlewoman	130
Chapter 15	Tabernacle	143
Chapter 16	Holyfolk	151
Chapter 17	Golden Hannah	162
Chapter 18	Faraway Shore	175
Chapter 19	City	184
Chapter 20	Ancient Mother	195
Chapter 21	Thief	209
Chapter 22	Russet Hannah	219
Chapter 23	Treasure at the Heart of the Tanglewood	232

Treasure at the Heart of the Tanglewood

Chapter I
Brown Hannah

Brown Hannah dwelt at the verge of the Tanglewood. The Tanglewood rose dark and deep. Heaths and moorland stretched to the southeast, scrub barrens to the north. A few poor cottars scratched out meager livings roundabout, mostly cutting peat. The Tanglewood ignored them, standing starkly aloof by a silvery shore. Limitless gray ocean rolled away to the west. A handful of fisherfolk plied its cold, thin waters.

Sometimes, in the far distance past sunset's haze, Hannah thought she spied lofting cloud. Uplands? An isle? She could not be sure. She herself had never strayed even so far as half a furlong from the margin of the Wood. Those timid souls who, now and again, crept up from the village to forest's edge could not tell her. They snatched her remedies with hurried thanks and made haste away, crossing their fingers against misfortune and murmuring luck charms beneath their breath. They deemed her Wood an enchanted place.

Folk said a fabulous treasure lay at its heart, a noble captive of high esteem; or a miraculous, fragrant, flowering tree; a staff of power; or a strange, unearthly beast, half horse, half stag, with a single, spiral horn thrusting up from its brow. Hannah laughed at their talk. She had never seen any prisoners or marvels within the Wood, only verdigris lichen frosting barren trees' bark, great ragged rings of burnished-bronze mushrumps stinking like cheese, mudmanders slick as new-whelped pups, and velvet moss softer than green herons' down.

"Ack! What a midden stench," cawed Magpie, skimming through the clearing's gloom to alight on Brown Hannah's shoulder.

The girl smiled, straightened; the many tattered layers of her dun-colored garment rustled like reeds. Her long hair fell tangled and fair, full of leaves and shoots and bits of twig. She pulled a few strands back from one cheek to glance sidelong at the bird.

"You know you love them roasted."

Hannah brushed damp earth from the smooth, crumpled cap of the mushrump she had just plucked. Her particolored companion humphed, feet like little rosebarbs pricking.

"Careful," Magpie instructed, bobbing. "Bruise it and the flesh will ruin."

"Why even pother with roasting?" Old Badger inquired. Sprawled at Hannah's feet, he nibbled at a dark golden stalk poised delicately between stubby black forepaws. "I savor them fresh from the soil."

The brown girl laughed wryly, nudged him with her toe. "Leave a few for the rest of us—" she started, but a flurry of coppery pelts and charcoal limbs and growling barks arrested her thought. Three half-grown fox pups hurtled into the glade. Rolling and tussling, they collided with the mushrump ring and trampled its morsels to pasty bits, which smirched the bright henna of their coats.

"Fleawits," Badger grumbled, lumbering to shelter in Hannah's lee.

"Curs!" Magpie shrieked, diving at them. "You'll not set one paddy-paw indoors this night. Off! Be off, you malodorous little mongrels."

Hooting and yapping, the three young foxes scattered. Off into the trees they streaked, Magpie darting behind. Holding back a sigh, Hannah turned from the mess and dropped her last mushrump into her withy basket.

"Well enough," she said to Badger. "The basket's full, and so's your belly. The morn grows late. We'd best fare home."

The old beast waddled portly in her wake as the brown-garbed girl stepped once more into the Tanglewood. The murk of the trees made Hannah shiver. The trail felt clammy beneath her bare footsoles. Breeze wuthered chill through the dense, leafless branches overhead. What chinks of sky showed through were iron gray.

"Badger," she asked after a time, "where'd you dwell once, before you came to this Wood?"

The ancient brock waggled his gray-wealed head.

"Don't know, girl," he panted. "With the years, I've grown so doddy . . . I can't recall."

Hannah stooped to heft the wheezing old thing into her arms. He settled his chin upon her shoulder with a whuff. Sturdy nails tapped lightly against her collarbone.

"Sometimes when I'm digging," he murmured, "it seems I almost recollect. . . . Or sometimes, when I catch a whiff of dung. . . ." He snorted. "I don't know why."

Hannah stroked his coarse, hoary fur. "Magpie isn't so venerable as you," she mused. "Yet she doesn't remember, either. Why's that?"

Badger sniffed and blew, snuffled and flew, in a rhythm that grew steadily slower and more content. Hannah tickled him between the shoulder blades.

"Strange, don't you think?"

Old Badger did not reply. His massy head lolled heavily against her. Wind rose, soughing through close-knit timber. The sheer, fawn-colored tissue of Hannah's gown riffled around her. She heard the foxlets' harking in the distance, intermingled with scolding Magpie's cries. Badger shifted. His snores grew sonorous. Hannah kissed his brindled pate then strode on along the path toward the edge of the Tanglewood.

When Hannah reached her rush hut on the Woodland's marge that noon, she found a little clutch of cottars waiting: an old man, two women, and a babe. Catching sight of her, they murmured, shawls clutched about the women's throats, cap gripped awkwardly in the gnarled man's hands. They watched intently, yet furtively, as Brown Hannah laid slumbering Badger beside his den, stowed her basket within the hut, then crossed to where the cottars stood to see what they would have of her.

Words came haltingly, their heads bowed low. Their eyes strayed nervously to the Tanglewood. First to step forward was the woman whose babe had a poxy rash. Hannah listened as the other described her daughter's night sweats and colic. When the woodland girl bent to loosen the bundling rags, she found a deep flush striating the little girl's breast. She stood a moment, lost in thought, clearing her mind of all other distraction, until it came to her exactly what needed to be done. Lightly, Hannah blew on the fretting child's forehead until she slept, then pulled some mustard greens and camphor twigs she found tucked in among her locks. They slipped free without a twinge.

"The mustard's for salve," she said, placing both into the mother's poke, "and the camphor to steep. Swab her chest thrice daily with the camphor tea and use the plaster tonight and tomorrow eve. You remember how?"

"Aye, miss," the woman whispered. "You healed my eldest of the same ill five years since."

She fell back hastily, shrinking from Hannah's touch, and nudged her companion forward. The young matron, lately delivered, had no milk to her teats. Weeping, she said her cousin had taken her newborn away yesternight to wet-nurse, lest he die. Hannah eyed the other's bony wrists and hollow cheeks, the dark smudges beneath her eyes.

"You shouldn't have come," the brown girl murmured, almost to herself.

The other's glance leapt up, stricken. "Had to, miss! He's my only babe. I can't just let another have him. You must help me get him back, help me feed him—"

Hannah clasped the young woman's hand in hers. "Of course I'll help you," she answered firmly. "Be at ease. I only meant you should have sent another in your stead."

The young matron's frame racked and trembled. Fiercely, she shook her head. "I've none. My man died. The others, my kith—they're all afraid."

Hannah felt her own brow furrow into a frown. "Afraid?" she asked, bewildered. "Of what?"

"Oh! Not you, miss," the other gasped, clutching her shawl as though she longed to break free, to run. "'Tis . . . the Wood. Just the Wood."

Hannah patted the other's freezing hand. "Nonsense," she exclaimed. "I venture the Wood daily and find no harm. It yields my livelihood, holds nothing to fear."

The young matron swayed, her face colorless. Alarmed, the brown-garbed girl steadied her. "Wait here," she said. "I have what you need inside."

From the hut, Hannah fetched a haversack woven of wild sheep strands gleaned from meadow thorns. Slitting the long, narrow poke down its seams, she lapped it loosely about the young matron's ribs and shoulders. Presently, the young woman's shivering ceased. Hannah packed a birchbark box with milkbud shoots and bits of silvery curlymoss from her hair, two little sacks of amber acorn flour from the storage chest beside the hearth, a handful of herbs, and a wax-dipped slab of tallowy fat-root she had been keeping in a bucket of branch water since the day before.

"Eat all of this by tomorrow night," she told the young woman. "Don't share a speck with your timid kith."

Magpie glided out of the Tanglewood to perch on Brown Hannah's shoulder, the long plumes of her tail tickling the girl's elbow. Hannah caught sight of her fox pups at the Wood's edge. One shook himself, raising a fine, damp spray; another ducked, while the third sat down with a thump and sneezed.

"Wantons," muttered Magpie. "Chased them twice across the ford, and still they reek." Teasing a broken shoot from Hannah's straw-colored locks, she began pecking the wispy thing to shreds. "What does this lot want?"

The cottars stood staring like startled mice.

"Peace, Magpie," Hannah hissed.

The pied bird laughed uproariously and shrugged. "What matter if I chatter? They won't grasp a thing I say." She spat the shoots out and turned to the village folk. "Will you?" she demanded, ignoring Hannah's shushing. The cottars glanced uneasily at one another. "Scullions!" Magpie called. "Even this tender slip of a girl kens my speech. Why can't you?"

The sleeping child began to whimper. The milkless young matron stood rigid as a deer. With a snort, Hannah swept Magpie from her shoulder and tossed her into the air.

"Away, you silly thing. I've folk to tend."

Squawking, the pied bird circled the yard, alighted at length on the rush hut's peak, where she perched, clucking and preening. The cottars gazed up at her without so much as a flicker of comprehension crossing their drawn and weary faces. Hannah blushed.

"Pay her no heed, I pray you. She means no ill."

The two women with the child had edged away. The old man stood foremost now. Hesitantly he came forward, clutching his cap.

"I want a curse, miss," he piped, eyeing Magpie.

Hannah's jaw dropped.

"To do my neighbor a mischief," he rattled on, wincing when Magpie cawed. "A mortal mischief, aye." Hannah drew herself up. "All in a just cause, miss," he added hastily, catching sight of the healer's stance. "None other, I swear."

Hannah folded her arms. The old man flinched. She felt her mouth grown hard. "Do you think I grant my boons for spite?"

"You'll not be the loser, miss," the old man insisted in a rush.

He held up a jingling bag of the round, brownish metal cottars sometimes tried to give her. Hannah turned away, but the villager ducked after, planting himself in her path.

"I'll settle you well. I'm a moneyed man—" He leaned toward her, still shaking his proffered payment.

"Fie!" Hannah spat and struck his hand aside.

In a flash, the fox pups sped across the yard and leapt to snatch the fallen purse. Romping and snarling, the three of them tore the soft, stitched leather apart. With a cry, the old man scrambled to retrieve his tokens as they rolled and strewed. Hannah watched him, furious.

"Leave me," she told him evenly.

"Nay, miss!" the cottar cried, running his fingers

through the dust. "You must curse him. He's a rogue—much younger than I. I'm no match. . . ."

The old man thrust a last handful of coin and dirt back into his cap. Still kneeling, he held it up.

"I've more, miss. More of this. I never pay tax, see? I'll fetch it—"

"Enough!" the fair-haired girl burst out. With a yelp, the old man subsided. "No more," she told him, "or the curse you'd lay upon your neighbor shall fall to you."

The old man gaped. The foxlets, still struggling over scraps, chased hither and fro across the yard. The cottar turned to the two village women, but both looked away. His hands tightened on the bits of metal bunched in his cap, twisting the fabric forlornly. The woodland girl said nothing more. The other opened his mouth as though to speak, hesitated, drew breath, then let it go again in a heavy sigh. Stiffly, he rose, bowed once to Hannah, then turned to shamble away toward the moorlands. The young healer watched his stooped retreat. Before her, the two women stood trembling, one distractedly soothing her drowsing child, the other weeping silently.

"There, Jenna," the older murmured to her companion. Then earnestly to Hannah, "We warned him not to ask, miss. Begged him. Pray don't be wroth with us."

Flushed, Hannah wrapped her arms about her waist, contrite. "I may be wroth," she answered softly, "but not with you. You came to me for healing, not for harm."

Both women smiled weakly, visibly relieved. The younger knelt to unbuckle her hamper.

"We'll be off then, miss," she said. "Pray you take these with our thanks."

Hannah waved the scrapple and bannocks away. "I've vittles enough." She gazed once more to the fleeing figure of the old man, nearly running now. The foxlets had launched themselves after him, nipping at his heels. Hannah whistled them off. "But tell me," she asked of the two women, "why would he wish his neighbor harm?"

Her fox pups trotted up to her. She knelt to stroke them, abruptly straightened and shooed them away. "Off. The lot of you stink."

"For courting his grandniece," the older of the two women replied. Her companion hastily rebuckled the hamper. "My mother knows the girl," the first woman continued. "The old miser wants to keep her till she's withered past wedding."

"What age is his niece?" Hannah asked.

"Nineteen years, miss," the younger woman answered, "so she's near beyond courting. I'm not seventeen myself."

"His niece lives with him?" Hannah asked. "Is she his housekeeper?"

The young matron nodded. Her companion snorted. "Slave, more like, miss," she added. "When she weds, he'll be alone—and his own doing, too. Driven off all other friends and kinsfolk long since."

Hannah watched the bent form of the old man, surprisingly spry for his years, dwindling with distance as he neared the moors. Sadly, she wondered what she must have done, years upon years since, to drive away all her own kith and relations—so far in the past now she could not even remember them. Behind her, she heard Badger wake and scratch his cheek. Magpie fluttered long-tailed from the roof to pester him. The two village women fidgeted, anxious to be gone. Hannah brought her gaze back to them as the old man entered the tossing heath.

"Return to me in four days' time," she bade them, "if the child's no better, or the milk hasn't come."

Chapter 2
Wizard

Hannah sat within her rush hut in the dimness of early afternoon. The walls of the place were translucent brown as onionskin, as the leaves of her gown. The withy basket of stinking mushrumps sat untended by the door. Magpie flitted about the yard, snapping at creeping things. Badger rested beside his den, while the foxlets chased, scrapping and dodging, along the verges of the Wood. A bowl of water on the table before her reflected her own image back at her. Hannah gazed down at the wan, disheveled girl looking out of the bowl.

Her long hair, fine and pale as flax, was full of the buds of crocuses and larkspur. They sprouted there, among the leafy shoots of other verdant things. They always had. Yet none of the starving cottars who came to her for remedies possessed such sprigs. Beneath their caps and kerchiefs, Hannah had ever glimpsed only shag like that of Blonde Grizzled Bear, or sheep's wool ringlets, or fine, plush nap like an otter's undercoat. It baffled her, and troubled her. Why should other human folk grow hair alone, while she grew more? Hannah peered uneasily at the nascent flowers and stalks forming among her locks. She knew she must pull them before they bloomed.

With a bitter sigh, Hannah rose and poured the water into an iron kettle. The villagers had disquieted her with their talk of mothers and cousins, of nieces and neighbors and courting. Hannah knew little of such matters, only what she had gleaned over many years from the cottars themselves. She hung the kettle from the hearth hook, poked at the coals beneath. Why would a man seek to hold a maid against her will? Why ask Hannah's aid to harm her suitor? Frowning, the brown girl shook her head. Such things were as mysterious to her as herbcraft seemed to these villagers.

A wisp of steam rose from the kettle. Carefully, biting her tongue, Hannah jerked out the buds nestling amid her tresses. The sprigs were green, deeply rooted. Each yank made her whole scalp ache. Hannah found herself panting, struggling against tears. She shut her eyes, working by feel. When nothing but hair remained and the bowl before her stood brimming with tender foliage, the brown-garbed girl stood gripping the table's edge, her knees locked. She sank down and laid her cheek against the surface of hard, smooth boards till the hiss of boiling kettle roused her.

Dizzily, Hannah dashed scalding water over the shoots, watched them shrivel and blanch. The steaming liquid darkened. She drained it into a covered goblet carved with runes she could not read. Still unsteady on her feet, she ducked through the doorway. Without, Magpie, Badger, and the fox pups halted, their eyes trailing her as she crossed the yard. Though Hannah never turned, clasping the goblet carefully in both hands, she sensed the others watching. None said a word or made move to follow. She felt glad for that. Reaching the trees, she found the path and turned her steps toward the forest's heart.

⊸━━━━⊷

The trek was crooked, long and weary, the afternoon spinning on toward eventide. Hannah made what speed she might through twisted treeboles and gray-green, leafless, clutching branches. The lidded flagon of tea smoked in her grasp. Despite her exertions, the healer girl shivered. She felt weak and drained. The foggy damp that pooled about the roots of the trees grew thicker and more chill the deeper into the Wood she fared. She set her teeth to keep them from chattering. The silence about her yawned cavernous.

Brown Hannah came to the crux of the Tanglewood, where her path and many others crossed and recrossed in a labyrinthine snarl. Not a thimbleful of light leaked through, the trees loomed and crowded so. The place was dark as dusk. Before her crouched a massive chair carved in runes like those upon the covered cup she bore. Nearby splayed a trestle-and-board table, laid with geared instruments for navigation at sea and the charting of stars. A set of standing shelves hoarded clay jars and beakers of clear, blown glass, some filled with clouded serums or pale tinctures. Three mortars and a pestle squatted on a low bench, a tiny scale poised delicately beside. Hammers, tongs, and a crucible bestrewed a burnt-out forge, its fires long spent.

No one was about. Brown Hannah waited. Mist curled, condensing upon her. Numbing silence rang in her ears. At last she heard a brisk, sure tread. A figure emerged from the gloom, a tall man, past middle years, but still straight and spare. Richly robed in shimmering samite embroidered with golden thread, he strode toward Hannah. Garnets adorned the robe's collar and sleeves. Carbuncles encrusted its hem. Gray scarcely leavened the dark gold of his well-trimmed beard, barely salted the temples of his coarse, straight hair. Smiling, he opened his arms to her.

"Well, slip," he said warmly. "I'd nearly given you up." His embrace crushed the tattered brown sheath against her, constricting her ribs. "Have you brought my draught?"

"Yes, Wizard," Hannah gasped. Stumbling back, she held the flagon up.

"Ah."

The Wizard smiled approvingly. Wresting it from her, he lifted the lid. A chuckle resounded in his chest. His teeth gleamed as he inhaled the steam. Hefting the flagon to his lips, he drained it in one eager draw. A deep sigh burst from him. His eyes brimmed. Color burned his cheeks. His golden beard seemed to glow more brightly, the radiance of his robe enrich, his blood-bright jewels glimmer more gorgeously.

"Splendid. Deliciously made." He pressed the goblet back to her. "Accept my thanks."

Hannah stood a moment, marshalling her wits. In the

Wizard's presence, she always felt slight, inconsequential—of as little import as a withy or a weed.

"Cottars came," she ventured, "this noon. . . ."

Smiling, the Wizard gazed down at her. "Did they mouth the same mutter they always do?"

Hannah hesitated, nodded. "They spoke of kin and neighbors—"

His chortle cut her off. "Tender bud, will you never heed?" He seized her arm and shook her. "You mustn't pay these worldly cottars any mind! They drudge about their dreary lives, getting and bearing, aging and dying. They don't live as we do, chit, safe in our Wood."

Hannah rubbed her arm. She eyed the closed flagon in her hand, the endless pattern of circling runes.

"Cottars grow nothing but hair on their heads," she said softly.

This time, the Wizard's mirth was a guffaw. "Oh, yes they do! It's just that you don't see it." He pulled Hannah closer to him. "Unlike you, my disheveled waif, villagers keep their pates neatly weeded."

She felt the slight, uncomfortable pulling as the other rolled a lock of her yellow hair between thumb and forefinger.

"But what ails them?" she asked, standing perfectly still. Struggle would avail her nothing. "They don't speak the tongue of animals or ken the craft of roots and herbs."

The Wizard loosed Hannah's hair with a snort. "No. They're witless brutes. The gift of magic's not for them."

"They come to me for charms," Hannah said. As soon as the words left her lips, she was sorry.

Scowling, the Wizard folded his arms, fingers tapping

against his sleeve. "I've bidden you before, lass, leave mag-icking to me. You're far too callow. You'll only come to grief."

He shook one finger at her sternly.

"Let those villeins find their own cures. Their trials are beneath your concern."

Hannah looked down, sighed heavily, as much with weariness as with rue. "But they seem . . . so sad."

The other harumphed. "Slaves to family and kith."

The brown-garbed girl studied her toes, which were blue with cold. "I have no kith, no family."

"You have me," the other snapped.

Unbidden, Hannah's voice continued, so soft she herself could scarcely hear it. "Nor neighbors. Nor suitors—"

"And should rejoice!" the Wizard exclaimed in disgust. "Sheltered by this Wood, fending for yourself, spared all ties of blood and entanglements of the heart—your life's so much freer, so much finer than the . . ." He seemed to grope for a phrase sufficient to convey his contempt. "Than the piteous subsistence of grubbers such as they!"

Hannah swallowed against the tightness in her throat.

"Their lives are so hard," she began, stopped. The Wiz-ard took her shoulders brusquely.

"You mustn't question," he pronounced. "Savor this haven instead. I myself once lived beyond—out there in the world—and mark me, it wasn't a merry place."

Hannah held her tongue. Mist ghosted gray about her feet. On the ground before her, the Wizard's slippers had pointed, slightly upturned toes, stitched with scenes of swine in gold filament, tossing dogs and trampling hunts-men. She had never noticed that before.

"Off now," he said, turning her toward the path down which she had come. "Much as I dote on you, I've weighty matters to attend."

He steered her swiftly to where the path slipped between the trees, muttering, "Wizard's work is never done."

Putting one hand to the small of her back, he gave Brown Hannah a firm little shove.

"Skip home to your herbs and your animals, sprig. We'll prat again next month when you bring my draught."

⟨✦⟩

By the time she returned to her rush hut at Wood's edge, the cloud-locked sun had long since sunk away. A fine drizzle fell hissing, almost sleet. Her loose, layered garment shed the weather like withered leaves. As she stumbled through the hut's doorway, nearly dropping with fatigue, she found Magpie had plucked each of the mushrumps from the basket and laid them neatly on the table. Badger had wrestled the roasting pan from its hook and dragged it onto the hearthstone to warm.

The healer girl gasped her thanks as she set the Wizard's rune-worked flagon alone upon its shelf. Weak, her head reeling, Hannah drank three long, cool dippers of rainwater from the bucket by the door. After her head had cleared a little, she placed the mushrumps in the pan, brushed them with oil, sprinkled them with herbs and sea salt, and stationed them on the coals to roast. Magpie sat beside her ear, nattering instructions. When the dish was done, the mushrumps had lost their stench and grilled to a buttery turn. Magpie pecked her gently on the cheek.

"There, you see? Under my wing, after all these years, you're becoming a passable cook."

Hannah smiled wanly. The tender flesh of the mushrumps warmed the hollow inside her. She dished ample helpings to the others, including the fox pups, who hardly stank at all now and toward whom Magpie had, on a full stomach, relented. They dozed in a heap beside the hearth, bellies taut as pilgrim drums. Badger lay nearby, flat and woolly-matted as a goatskin. Magpie breasted on a roof beam overhead, tail feathers streaming, bill snugged beneath one pinion. Hannah banked the coals. Dry and warm and well-fed now, she felt her head still throbbing. She ran weary hands through the fox pups' fur. They yawned and rolled. The girl bent to kiss snoring Badger on the nose, stood on tiptoe to smooth her fingers lightly over Magpie's down, before curling into exhausted slumber on the soft folds of her rush tick.

When morning broke dull and gray and cold, she felt little refreshed. Cloud cover had thickened. The dank air bit deeper, to the bone. A succession of days crawled past, each starkly somber as the last. Brown Hannah dragged herself shivering through the scrubbing of cookpots under Magpie's pert eye; the digging of roots alongside Badger, some to boil, some to cellar, and some to bed in the garden plot; the collecting of deadwood with the foxlets to keep the hearth fire bright.

No cottars came, but the woodland girl treated titmice

with frostbitten wings, an otter who had cut his elbow on a root, a deer who had wedged a stone in one hind hoof, then walked on it until it had worn the flesh raw. In order to ease the afflictions of any creature that came, Hannah gave whatever she could from the smattering of healing plants she found once more gradually beginning to nestle in among the hairs of her temples, nape, and crown. As always, she had only to clear her mind, calm her heart, and think deeply for a few moments to know just what remedy would suffice.

Unlike human visitors, the animals neither asked for things beyond reason nor offered gifts in thanks—yet Magpie had as little to do with them as she did with cottars, calling them all beggars and riffraff. The only forest creature to whom she accorded even grudging respect was Blonde Grizzled Bear, enormous and ponderous, who lumbered up one day with a honey-smeared snout and badly beestung ears.

Badger was more charitable toward their fellow inhabitants of the Wood, despite the difficulty in carrying on much conversation with them. They seemed to have rather simpler wits than either Magpie or Badger, a circumstance the young healer had never found surprising because it had always been thus. The fox pups, of course, were eager to have a game out of any animal that approached the rush hut— and were not above trying to eat some of the smaller rodents and birds. One afternoon, Hannah had to be very stern with all three over bullying a family of mite-infested minks, who were in no mood.

At last, in time, the chill weather eased, the dismal overcast beginning to lift and thin toward a clearer sky. The now leafy-haired girl felt her strength slowly start to revive, the sap rising in her veins as the shoots and buds among her locks commenced once more to grow more hardily. Time dragged on, as it always had, one day very much like the one before it as Hannah went about her accustomed rounds.

Sometimes, gleaning and gathering, she found round hoofprints deep in the Wood: the tracks of great horses, heavy-shod. They came from the steeds of knights-errant, she knew. Year after years, these young men-at-arms came, their blank shields burnished bright as dinner plate. Some tall, some burly, strapping as oxen or lean as hounds. Few so much as spared her a glance as they coursed on by on their long white horses. Some she recalled distinctly: one a ginger-haired boy, close-cropped curls bobbing about his ears, and another, a great while after him, a long-faced lad with freckled cheeks. She had no idea why they entered the Tanglewood. Sometimes, days later, their horses limped out again. The young knights themselves never did.

One morning, walking through high ferns at Wood's edge, beneath a sheer veil of cloud through which burned glimpses of blue, Hannah came across fresh trampled bracken. Glancing down its passage, she caught a flash of white flanks and vivid caparison: a young knight on his destrier, loping away from her, into the trees.

"Hold!" Hannah shouted, casting off the bulky bundles of thatch she carried and dashing in his wake. "No path traverses the Tanglewood! The trees twine more densely the deeper one goes. Its heart is impassable. Turn back!"

Breathless, pulse pounding, she stumbled to a halt as horse and rider vanished into the Wood. The young man did not turn. She never saw his face, only his nut-brown hair, long as a mare's mane, flying behind him as he disappeared beneath the forest's looming shadow. The pummel of hoof-beats faded from the air. Hannah stood panting, her throat tight. What use to call, to try to stay them? None ever paused or made reply. They seemed to pay her no more heed than one might a tree.

Silently, she retrieved her bundled thatch. What drove these riders—or drew them—here? What did they hope to accomplish in the Wood? She fingered the twist of grass that bound her thatch. The Wizard had warned against useless pondering. Yet she wondered still. Frowning, Brown Hannah hoisted her burden again, balanced it cumbrously across one shoulder. Her thoughts shifted, seeking, unanswered, as she turned once more, trudging on through the bracken toward home.

Chapter 3
Rumors

When Hannah reached her hut in the hour before noon, she found Badger holed deep in his den, Magpie flown, and the fox pups off about their own business. A band of cottars stood huddled beside her herb trellis, the first she had seen in many days. Two men and a boy this time, and two young women besides. Hannah nodded in greeting, then hauled the thatch inside to stow among the roof beams before returning to the villagers in the yard.

The least reluctant to present himself was the man whose son had a stye. After a few moments of careful reflection, Hannah cleaned the lad's eye with well water and squeezed three drops of haresblink onto the spot. Pulling more of the brittle, juicy herb from her hair, she gave it to his father and bade him do the same morn, noon, and eventide until the sore shrank away. The peat cutter came forward next, holding a gashed forearm. The brown-garbed girl bathed and stitched it, then wrapped it in a dressing of woundwort. To the maid who hemmed and stammered, she gave a kernel of spice and a sprig of fragrant peppermint to chew. Last to speak was the other maid, whose sullen mien and pouting lip marred otherwise comely features. She bobbed a curtsy and muttered: "I'd ask a charm, miss."

"What manner of charm?" Hannah replied, noting the maid's furtive glance over one shoulder toward the peat cutter.

"A charm for love, miss," the sulky maid hissed. "I'm unlucky there. The man I want, see—he doesn't favor me."

Hannah saw the peat cutter, who gazed pointedly away across the heath, heave a short, silent sigh. Beside him, the father and the other maid stood, biting down smiles. The eyes of the sulky maid flashed, and she wheeled as though to rail at them—but catching sight of Hannah's upraised brows, she held her peace.

"You must help me, miss, or I'll go distracted! Every lackwit in the village'll have me a laughingstock else."

The woodland girl considered. A plan bloomed in her mind. "Well enough," she said at last, teasing a supple strip of finely fringed whisperfern from her hair. It was nearly as long as one of Magpie's tailfeathers. Hannah knocked the spores off. "Put this down your bodice."

"What?" the village girl exclaimed, and then, plainly aghast at her own outburst, seized the feathery leaf and thrust it quickly between the lacings at her throat. "I mean, aye, miss."

She stood fidgeting.

"Don't scratch it," Hannah said.

"Nay, miss," the girl replied, snatching her hand away.

Hannah watched her color rise. "Does it tickle?"

"Horribly!"

Brown Hannah nodded. "Each time you feel it prick, you must say silent to yourself: 'Hard words win no hearts.'"

The village girl stared at her.

"Do this for one turning of the moon."

The other nodded uncertainly.

"One more thing," Hannah told her. "How do you make your living?"

"Cook, miss," she murmured, puzzled.

"Then each day, bring the man you favor some morsel made by your own hand for him alone. Can you do that?"

"I can try, miss," the other answered. Her eyes turned openly toward the young man now. He stood gazing back at her cautiously.

"The fern won't work unless you do the rest," Hannah added.

The maid mulled on it. "Aye," she announced suddenly. "I can do it. I shall."

She opened her poke, and the others their haversacks, offering Hannah peat bricks and charcoal along with their thanks. The fair-haired girl shook her head.

"No need. I've ample fuel already for my fire. But tell me this: did any of you see a young knight this morning?"

Again she thought of him, and again the sensation filled her of shouting after one riding heedless away. A flush warmed her cheeks. She blinked and shook herself. The cottars stood before her still. Only the maid who had stammered so spoke.

"I m-might have seen him, miss. From a distance, early this morn. Was he clad in bright lake, his mount hoary as rime?" She smiled to herself, clearly pleased at the words' coming easier now. "But he nor stayed nor spoke to me."

Brown Hannah sighed. "How long have they come," she wondered aloud, "these strange questers on white horseback?"

A doubtful silence. "Long as I or anyone remembers, miss," the man who had brought his son replied.

"But why?" Hannah exclaimed, more to herself than to them. She remembered the drumming of hooves drawing farther and farther away until the Wood muffled all sound into nothingness. A scuffling of feet among the cottars then, a clearing of throats.

"Well, treasure, miss," said the maid unlucky in love. "To free the lovely hostage whose dowry's worth the world's ransom. . . ."

"Be off," the young man beside her scoffed. "The treasure's no virgin. 'Tis a tree that fruits riches—"

"Nonesuch!" exclaimed the father of the boy. "'Tis a magical mooncalf. . . ."

"A 'chanter's wand!"

Hannah found herself laughing, half at their absurdity, half in despair. "But there's nothing! Not one thing such as those to be found in the Wood. Who tells them so?"

Silence. Shrugging.

"Tales spread," murmured the young woman whose breath now savored of peppermint and clove.

Before them, the brown-garbed girl shook her head. "Where do they come from, these nameless youths?"

Another silence.

"One stopped the night at my nan's house once," the pouty maid with the fern down her bodice ventured at last. "Said he came from 'cross the sea. But he spoke near nary of it, and so oddly too, as like he couldn't quite recall. Nan thought him a smack touched in the head."

Hannah fingered the loose, worn tatters of her gown. "Do none ever emerge?"

The cottars murmured, studied one another till the boy with the stye breathed softly, "Da says the Golden Boar brings every one of them to naught."

Sharp intakes of breath from the others, quickly stifled. Hannah saw widened eyes darting glances at the Tanglewood. The pouty maid hugged herself and shivered, while the peat cutter and the younger maid made furtive gestures with their hands, as though signing against evil. The older man shushed his son, drew him protectively against his side.

"We must depart, miss," he declared. "We leave these stores for you in thanks."

"No, wait," the young healwoman exclaimed as the five villagers edged hastily away. "I've no need of them. Hold a moment, I beg you. What is this you say of a Golden Boar?"

She could have sworn she knew every herb and wight that harbored in the Wood, but she had never before found sign or heard tale of any Golden Boar. She reached out toward the retreating villagers, but they dispersed, would not be stayed.

"We mustn't dally," they burst out, almost in chorus, like so many startled jays. "We'd not overstay our welcome—nor keep you from your work." Each gaze flitted fearfully between her and the Wood.

"Take your stores with you," Hannah called after them. "Use them to warm your own lodgings. I've plenty!"

But they were already scurrying toward the heath, their offerings abandoned. The farther from Hannah the villagers drew, the more their pace increased until the little cluster of cottars was hurrying along just short of a run. Hannah stared after them straggling swiftly across the moorland. Then her own eyes turned to the Wood behind, dark and cavernous even in the pale promise of sunlight just beyond the cloud. A gusting breeze from the southeast whistled and soughed. The brown girl wiped her palms on the dry, rustling foliage of her garment and turned back toward her rush hut.

"I'll ask Magpie and Badger and the fox pups," she vowed softly to herself. "When they return, I'll see what they can tell me of this Golden Boar."

<hr>

"Nothing!" screamed Magpie, fluttering about the thatch-strewn roof beams of the hut, incensed at having no perch left free on which to settle. "I know nothing of any Golden Boar. There isn't one—so best not go looking!"

She came to rest on the back of the chair, where she crouched polishing her bill against the wood's smooth edge. Brown Hannah frowned. She sat on the hut's dirt floor, lacing hanks of thatch into sheaves with which to patch the thin places in her roof and walls. Badger sat beside her, combing his claws through the little heap of reeds in his lap.

"If ever I heard of a Golden Boar, I've forgotten it long

since," Badger murmured. "Surely no such thing exists. Magpie and I'd have told you if it did."

Hannah eyed him dubiously. She realized the bunch she had just tied was too small, unwrapped the grass twine, added to the clump and began again.

"Hark!" the fox pups laughed at her from the doorway. "Hoof. Harry. Woof! Warp!" One of them began worrying the shuttle of the little hand loom on which she was weaving a new woolen sack. Hannah threw a handful of broom-corn at the trio.

"If neither of you knows," she said to Magpie and Badger, "then I must ask the cottars."

"Ha!" Magpie crowed, swooping to perch on Hannah's neatly stacked bunches of thatch. "You'll have forgotten all about it by the time another motley batch show themselves."

"I'll ask tomorrow," the brown-garbed girl replied, dropping her latest clump on top of the others so that Magpie had to flutter out of the way.

"How's that?" Badger asked as Hannah took the little sheaf he had gathered for her.

"I know very well where their village must lie," she answered, looping twine about the sheaf. "I've seen the path they trek."

"Nay!" Magpie squawked from the floor. "Child, you mustn't!"

Badger pawed lightly at her gown. "Hannah, how wise is this? The Wizard bade you truck no more with cottars."

The young healer shrugged, impatient. "So he has ever bidden."

"Mark me, the Wizard will be much peeved if you leave

the Wood," the pied bird warned, hopping and beating her wings against the hard-packed earth.

"Magpie," Hannah exclaimed, extending her hand. Magpie ignored the proffered perch, thrashing up dust in a passion. Hannah shook her head. "The Wizard doesn't care a whit what I do or where I go, so long as, month to month, I bring him his herbal draught."

The fair-haired girl peered sidelong at her own locks then, uneasily. Sheaths and panicles, tiny shoots and sprays of fragrant buds were beginning to peep through her tresses. A delicious vigor beat in her veins, making her bold. By rights she knew she ought to bring the Wizard his herb tea today, but the hut needed mending before the crisp air turned frigid again, and she would need her strength to take her to the village next morn. She resolved to prepare his tea tomorrow afternoon. He had never trifled to question her over the variance of a day or two.

"Sooth," Hannah murmured, stroking the coarse, silvery hair of Badger's head, "the Wizard pays me so little mind, I think he knows of my dealings only what I make bold to tell."

"Rubbish!" cawed Magpie. Seizing a cane straw from the pile, she began snapping it to pieces. Hannah reached after her, but she jigged away, clucking and chirring. Sighing, Brown Hannah rose.

"The cottars left their charcoal and peat," she said, hefting an armful of little bundles of thatch. "Surely the Wizard won't begrudge my returning it."

"Bosh!" Magpie sprang into the air and whipped through the door in such a rush it sent the foxlets scattering.

"You'll rue this," she called raucously from the yard. "No good can come of it!"

Hannah turned to Badger, who sat pensively licking one already fastidiously clean forepaw.

"Well," she said to him. "What do you think?"

"Sweet bud," he told her quietly, "I think your Wizard's not half so tender of heart as you."

Chapter 4
Village

The gorse swept and whispered around her; the humming heather broomed in the cool, stiff breeze as Brown Hannah made her way across the moor. Early morning sun, a shining haze in the east behind the racing veil of cloud, nearly warmed her as she strode. The sack of peat and the charcoal hod felt wonderfully wieldy and light. The Tanglewood, still visible in the distance behind her, dwindled with every step. The woodland girl shook her head and laughed. Green things in her hair riffled in the wind.

She came to a broad and dusty path. Following it, she saw a cottage, larger than her own, and woven of sticks. A man in shirtsleeves stood in the yard, splitting shingles with a hammer and wedge. Hannah was sure she did not know him. He had never come to her for a remedy. His back to her, he seemed intent upon his task.

Hannah traveled on, reluctant to intrude, passing other cots, some of sod, some of stone. She saw women with their hair in kerchiefs feeding pullets meal; a man toting a pail of milk, two boys, one with a cane pole, the other with a string of silvery fish. No one paid her any notice. Rounding a curve in the road, she found herself abruptly within a great cluster of huts, three dozen at least, and realized this must be the village proper.

People passed hither and fro across the open space between dwellings. Hannah set down her sack and scuttle. In the distance, two children chased after a cat. She thought one of them might have been the lad she had treated for a stye. A young woman emerged from the hovel nearest Hannah, turned and walked three houses down to where a man stood waiting. When he held out his arms, she ran the last few paces to him and kissed his cheek. Hand in hand, the two set off.

Hannah became aware then of a bent figure who had also just come from the near hut. He stood staring sourly after the pair. Turning on his heel to re-enter the house, he caught sight of Hannah and staggered back. Horror swept the creases of his face. The fair-haired girl realized only then that he was the old man who had come to her a moon ago, seeking a hex to harm the suitor of his niece. With a cry, the cottar stumbled into his hut and shoved shut the door. As Hannah drew near, she heard an iron bolt drawn into place.

"Old man," she exclaimed, thumping the door with the heel of her hand. "Come out. I seek a word with you."

"Spare me!" The thickness of the door muffled his reedy wail. "I've done naught to stand between them. I swear!"

Hannah thumped the door again. "I've no doubt," she answered. "But it isn't regarding that matter that I've come."

The sound of scraping and of scrabbling within, as of some table or chest being pushed into place athwart the door.

"I've not prevented her, miss! She goes to him whenever she wills. They'll marry soon." The old man's words were full of terror. "All the village will vouchsafe me!"

"I beseech you, don't fear," the girl on the doorstep called to him. "I seek only to find those who left their charcoal and peat at my hut day past."

No answer then. No sound at all through the door but the old man's panting. Hannah shook her head in bewilderment.

"Peace," she said at last. "Know that I mean no harm to you or anyone."

Turning from the old man's door, she realized that some among the village had taken note of her now. A few stood halted upon the street, others staring from their windows. Many gazed in consternation, several in wonder, more still in alarm.

"The Damsel!" she heard them gasp.

"Look, 'tis the Damsel . . . the Damsel!"

"The Woodland Dame—"

"Why do you call me that?" the brown-clad girl asked a curly-haired young woman. "I call myself Hannah."

But the other only hurried off, her periwinkle smock beating blue in the wind. The fair-haired girl glanced down at her own faded shift, the color of old reeds. The only garment she owned, its countless translucent layers fluttered about her. She had worn it ever since her first recollection, that of waking in the Tanglewood, a stripling lass well able to skip and chat, to kindle fire with a fingersnap and gather her own dinner. The gown flared and settled, wispy and tattered as a winter rush, just as it had on that earliest day, when first she had opened her eyes and gazed about and known her own mind and named herself.

"Brown Hannah," she called after the retreating maid, who never turned.

Folk fell away from the woodland girl as she crossed back to the scuttle of charcoal and the bag of peat. Her long flaxen locks, full of shoots and leaves, tossed in the freshening breeze. Catching sight of her, a cartman leading a small dun ass hastily dragged the beast, wheezing and hawing, out of her path.

"What's amiss?" she asked, but the ass made no reply, trotting smartly after the man as he hustled it off. She heard thumping as some among the townsfolk pulled their shutters shut. Others merely continued to stare. One Hannah recognized, a woman standing in the doorway of a nearby cot. The bottom half of the door was latched, the top half inward-swung. The woman did not draw away as the outlander approached. The wind changed course. Hannah pushed at her wild cornsilk hair all unbound, discovering in dismay many of the buds there already opening.

"I know you, don't I?" she asked the woman at the door. "You came to me once with a broken bone."

"Aye, miss." The woman smiled, not the least bit disconcerted. "Many years ago."

Consternation swept over Hannah suddenly as she eyed the woman more closely now. "But what's become of you?" she exclaimed.

The other shook her head. "Naught, miss. I'm very well."

"But," said the brown-garbed girl, "your face, your hands. The color of your hair. . . ."

The woman touched the fine strands of dove-gray at her temples and laughed. "Hair fades," she said. "And wrinkles come with time. 'Tis only age, miss. I've borne and reared two daughters since last we met."

Brown Hannah stared at her, bewildered still. "But . . . why haven't I become as you?" she murmured. "You were a girl—scarcely older than I—when you brought your broken wrist to me."

The woman drew breath as though to speak, but a bustle within the house interrupted her. Another, younger woman with a child on her hip appeared in the doorway.

"Who is it, Mam? Who's at the door—"

Catching sight of Hannah, the other stopped short. The flower-haired girl discerned the woman who had come to her the previous moon with a sickly child. The little maid sat cheerly now, fingers curled about her mother's bodice, eyeing Hannah with interest. Another child, older, a boy, peered from around his mother's skirt. The brown girl smiled.

"Your youngest is better, I see."

"Aye, miss," the other whispered, dipping a curtsy to her. "Right as rootstock within the week I took her to you."

Hannah turned to the older woman. "And this is your daughter?"

Smiling, the other nodded. "One of them. . . ."

A second commotion within the house.

"Ilss! Becca." A man's voice called from within. "For

Lady's love. . . ." The two women parted. A gray-haired man, suddenly between them, clasped one arm about his wife's wrist, laid the other hand on his daughter's elbow. "Still yourselves! You mustn't keep her."

Turning toward Hannah, he bowed awkwardly.

"Please, miss. You must away, back to your Wood."

The outland girl studied his kind, nervous eyes and shaking hands. She knew she had never treated him for any ill. The child on his daughter's hip leaned out to him to be held. Without taking his gaze from Hannah, the old man took the little girl. His words were hurried.

"Be off, miss, I beg you, or the Golden Boar will come!"

Hannah stopped short.

"What is this Boar?" she asked him eagerly. "Cottars who came to me yesterday spoke of it and fled. Yet I know nothing of such a beast, though I've dwelt my whole life within the Wood."

The old man and his wife exchanged glances. Their daughter stroked her young son's head. Her father sidled, cleared his throat. The little girl patted the stubble of her grandfather's beard. Gently, his wife squeezed his arm and nodded. The old man licked his lips.

"It dwells in the heart of the Tanglewood, miss. A huge, fierce thing. Yearly we pay it tribute."

"Tribute?" Hannah murmured, testing the feel of the sounds on her tongue. She had never heard the word before. The old man let out his breath.

"Coin, miss. Any gem we might own—as though any remained!" He shifted the child to his hip. "Ore of precious metals, any pearl we might fish out of a stream."

Not understanding, Hannah drew breath to speak, but the man hurried on.

"But we've paid the year's ransom! In full, miss, just two moons past. I beseech you, tell your master the sum was meager only because we've no more to give—"

Once more the strong breeze gusted. Astonished, Hannah shook her head. Bees buzzed hungrily about her honey hair. She swatted at them distractedly.

"But I tell you, I know nothing of any Golden Boar," she protested. "I came only to return the charcoal and peat your fellows left at my hut yesternoon. . . ."

The old man's agitation increased. "But he wards you, miss, just as he wards the Wood. Don't you see? If he finds you strayed, he'll come searching, and if you lead him here, we'll pay not gold, but blood."

His tone made the fine hairs at the nape of Hannah's neck stand up, though she could make no sense of his words. Beside him, the man's wife took his arm.

"Generations past, miss," she said, "in my grandam's time, the Boar took more than tribute from us. I lost two uncles and my godmother to his teeth."

Hannah felt her skin shrink. "This Boar, are you saying he slew them?" she asked. The old woman nodded. "But why?"

"To feed upon, miss."

Hannah's gorge rose. She stared at the old woman—standing quietly, no longer smiling, but still calm—at her husband quaking beside her, at their silent daughter and two grandchildren, the littlest laughing, the boy silently watchful, all framed in the broad doorway. The girl from the Wood considered their words and could not find her tongue. Revulsion threaded like creepers through the narrow spaces of her bones.

"Now, of course," the gray-haired woman added quietly, "since my children's time, since the young knights have begun to come, the Boar asks only tribute of us."

"We would keep it so," her husband beside her whispered.

He handed his daughter her youngest child, who peered expectantly down her mother's bodice. The young woman kissed the little girl's head and curtsied once again to Hannah.

"Lady keep you, miss," she murmured.

Taking her son's hand, she turned and led him with her as she carried his sister from the doorway. The brown-garbed girl stared at the old couple who remained. Her hair was aswarm with nectar-sippers now: three bronze bees, a hawk moth, two velvet mead flies, and a handful of enormous, stingless honey wasps. The breath of lilies hung heavy on the air. From time to time, she glimpsed the cottars closing their eyes and breathing deep.

"Do you tell me all the young knights are devoured by the Boar? This is why none of you warn them from the Wood?"

"None m-might stay them, miss," a small voice alongside her said, "however he strove. We've tried."

Brown Hannah turned, surprised, to see one of the maids who had come to her the day before, the one who had stuttered so she could scarcely speak. Others of the villagers had crept closer as well. Among them, the woodland girl spied the young matron who had been unable to suckle her newborn child. Hannah's dark woolen sacking still lapped warmly about the other's torso. Her cheeks were fuller, blushed with rose. She held a bundle to one shoulder. Hannah heard an infant's gurgling sigh. The young mother's eyes met Hannah's. She said, "Those knights are all under some enchantment, miss. Nor word nor deed from any here might turn them from their quest."

A stout young man alongside her added earnestly, "The dairyman locked one in the cowshed once, a few years back, but he dug himself out and off he went, horse or no."

"Where do they come from?" breathed Hannah.

The maid with the savor of peppermint on her tongue answered, "F-faraway."

"Will you go now, miss?" the old man in the doorway begged. "Go and not return? If you bring the wrath of the Boar upon us, we're lost."

Hannah stood speechless. "Of course," she managed at last. "I ask only that yonder charcoal and peat be restored to its owners. The weather will turn cold again, this afternoon, most like. I beg you bring me no such precious gifts in future. I've no need of them. I give my remedies freely and ask nothing in fee."

As Hannah turned to step away from the hut, the cottars before her parted, but slowly this time, without shouts and scrambling. The wind had died. Behind her, she heard the old woman admonishing softly.

"Love, that was the Winter Damsel you spoke to so free. Does she not merit more gentleness?"

"I know it, Ilss," the old man sighed wearily. "I know it well. But what use, when the Boar holds her powerless as he does us all?"

Chapter 5
Tanglewood's Crux

Brown Hannah ran whole the way back from the village, across the sunny moors and rising uplands toward the Wood. It seemed no more than a double dozen strides before she reached the dark forest's edge. Yet she did not feel winded, so strongly did the sap of the green growth in her locks course through her. The brown-garbed girl forced herself to slow, to halt. The rush hut stood deserted. Neither Magpie nor Badger nor the foxlets were about. Scarce pausing, Hannah ducked through the entryway and snatched the carven goblet from its shelf. Bent trees reached toward her from the Wood.

Hannah dashed down the woodland path, sprinting headlong toward the heart of the Tanglewood. The leafless canopy of branches wove tighter and tighter overhead, screening the light. At last they closed entirely, blocking all sun so that Hannah sped through a gloaming heavy as gathering twilight, although in truth it was only just past noon.

The shady air chilled. Mist crept about the forest's knotted roots. The trees themselves thronged thicker the deeper into the darkling Wood she passed. Abruptly, she realized a firefly had found its way into the buds sprouting amid her hair. It clung there winking, illuminating the leafy shoots. She brushed it free and rushed on. Its candent light glimmered behind until she lost it in the fog.

Hannah came to the nexus where all paths of the Tanglewood converged. The Wizard's furniture stood strewn with his books and vials and instruments. The Wizard himself sat at table, bent over a gleaming golden plate richly wrought about the rim. One hand held a slender, two-tined fork, the other a poniard with a jeweled hilt. With short, swift strokes, he sliced a bit of whatever rested on his plate and popped it into his mouth. His yellow teeth bore down on it. The fair-haired girl stopped short, staring, surprised to find him already arrived. Always before, she had waited for him.

"Sprig!" the Wizard exclaimed. "There you are." He ground his morsel and swallowed. "You're late. What kept you?"

Hannah clutched the covered cup.

"Cottars," she stammered. "Villagers—they spoke of treasure, and of knights devoured by a Golden Boar. . . ."

The Wizard's eyes upon her sharpened. "Tad, didn't I expressly forbid you to truck with those churls?" He set down his cutlery. "Their heads are full of figments, and their tongues spout nothing but rot."

He fingered something on his plate in distaste. Hannah fidgeted. The Wizard had always been her touchstone, explaining away every troublesome quandary. Hannah tried to make out what it was he worried, but the distance, the mist, and the gloom were too great. He worked a tidbit free of the rest.

"But the knights . . ." she managed.

With a sigh, the Wizard tossed the thing, perhaps a bone, over one shoulder and away into the fog. The red jewels of his white robe sparkled as he rose.

"My simple, little poppet—of course the knights are real," he replied, approaching through the dark. "They aren't figments. You've seen them. So have I. Poor young fools seeking treasure."

He chuckled wryly.

"They never find it. No treasure lies within the Wood. And certainly no ravening boar."

The golden stitching of his robe glinted softly as he moved. The coarse, aurous hairs of his neat-trimmed whiskers were of almost exactly the same lustrous hue.

"Whenever I happen upon these errant souls, wandering lost, I guide them out of the Wood—though sometimes the timber brakes press so thick their horses can't get through."

He shrugged ruefully, drawing alongside Hannah.

"Indeed, rescuing young dunderheads consumes more time than I can easily afford. . . ."

His breath steamed in the cold. Hannah felt the hair along her arms stand up. She blushed, shivered, feeling his eyes directly upon her.

"But surely I've told you all this before?"

His voice was smooth, a silken stream. Mutely, the brown-clad girl shook her head. A tiny light flickered in the fog. Hannah realized her firefly had followed. Its meandering glow illuminated vague surfaces. Earthen mounds? Thickets of thorn? Scowling, the Wizard snapped his fingers. The firefly's nimbus abruptly vanished. Gray vapors poured across the spot where it had shone, obscuring even the faintest shapes from view. She heard the Wizard clear his throat.

"Now to task, sweet slip. I'll have my draught. It's a dry meal has no dram to chase it down."

He swept the cup from her. Lifting the lid, he froze, frowning down into its interior.

"Empty—"

His gaze flicked to Hannah. The fair-haired girl stared back at him. Only then did she realize that in coming directly from the village, without so much as a moment to collect her thoughts, she had paused at her rush hut only long enough to snatch the cup from its shelf, not steep the tea to fill it. Incredulity swept over her, and shame.

She managed only to stammer, "I forgot!"

The Wizard's eyes narrowed, gaze combing through her locks.

"Ah," he muttered, nodding to himself. "Now I see what's caused your wildness." One hand darted like a hawk's pounce to her hair. "Flibbertigibbet, why do you let these weeds grow? Haven't I warned you that, left unchecked, they'll addle your reason?" He grasped her firmly by one arm. "We must have them out!"

Hannah gave a startled cry as, in a passion, he began to pluck. The pulling, yanking, tearing jerked her this way and that. The pain's intensity astonished her.

"Your own fault," he chided sternly. "If only you'd culled them before, as I'd bidden, you wouldn't be in this misery."

His clasp was adamant, his fingers forcible. She could not have escaped him had she tried. Her ears rang, temples pounding as every shoot and stalk, blossom and twig rooted among her tresses was zealously seized and wrested, sometimes by twos and threes. She had to bite her lip to keep from screaming.

"Bear up," he admonished. "The sting will pass. Only in this way can I purge you of irksome humors. . . ."

Hannah found herself reeling, no longer supported. The Wizard had released her arm. Her splitting head felt hollow, light. Something cool and wet streamed from her scalp. She thought at first it was blood, recognized it only belatedly as sap, clear green and sweetly savored. She stared at the pale smears on her fingertips. It was difficult for her to see through the haze of pain. Tears coursed her cheeks. She realized she was gasping for breath.

"There," the Wizard said smartly. "I daresay you feel calmer now."

His words sounded as from a great distance away. Turning, dazed, Hannah beheld him not ten paces from her. An urn of silver floated in the cloudy brume before him. At his wave, a smoking stream spouted into the copper basin hovering below. Stems and stalks heaping the basin collapsed beneath the boiling rush. Its fragrance reached her. The Wizard inhaled the steam. He clapped his palms, and the basin tilted, disgorging its fluid contents into the runic wooden cup. The flowing tea fell dark, dark green. Dregs, basin, and urn all shimmered and evaporated as the Wizard signed them to be gone. He plucked the only vessel remaining, his carven goblet, from the air.

"What a fresh brew," he murmured joyfully. "Truly a potent dram. . . ."

Hannah staggered, mute, unable to catch either her balance or her breath. Fog swirled damp about her. Her skull hammered. Cool sap flowed down the back of her neck, chilling her spine. She felt groggy, weak. The ground leaned and shifted underfoot. Across from her, the Wizard quaffed his draught. He closed his eyes with a sigh. His ruddy complexion deepened. The jewels of his robe scintillated. His lungs drew vigorous inspirations. Hannah wiped the cold sap drenching her fingers onto the cool rustling tatters of her gown. The Wizard's eyes snapped open.

"Still here, chit? Run along," he bade her. "I must finish my meal."

He tossed the goblet at her. Hannah contrived to catch the heavy flagon just as it thumped her hard across the collarbone. She felt a bruise begin to rise. Turning away, the Wizard stopped short.

"You're weeping, elf?" he inquired. "Whatever for? I pruned that poisonous greenery only to shield you from harm."

Hannah could muster no reply. Her teeth chattered. Her knees shook. The Wizard seated himself before his plate.

"Get home to your own table, my floret," he called. "Come sooner to me next time and spare your pretty head."

Hannah's strength ebbed. She felt frozen, faint. Slicing another bite from his meat, the Wizard began to chew.

"And pay no more heed to those gossiping villeins!

Their Golden Boar's mere fancy. Trust me, frondling. Every knight who enters my Wood fares safely on his way."

Hannah barely managed a nod before turning from him and stumbling blindly away down the nearest path.

⌖

Brown Hannah tottered through the freezing mist. The pain in her head was agony. The air had turned pitch-black, bitterly cold. Shivering, she wondered how day could have turned to moonless night so soon. She leaned heavily for a long moment, panting against a tree, before struggling on, scarcely able to see for the gruel-thick fog. Nothing looked familiar to her. She felt as though she were rambling in circles, round and around the Wizard's lair. Never before in the maze of pathways merging at the heart of Tanglewood had she ever lost her way.

Hannah came to a place that was littered with bones. Before her, the heavy mist parted. Thickets of gorse lay crushed and torn, as by the rootings of some prodigious beast. Great ruts gouged the soil, left by massive hooves. The tree boles were all scraped and scarred, as from the polishing of mighty tusks. Beyond, through the thinning fog, Hannah caught glimpses of something more. She moved haltingly forward until she found herself among head-high heaps of glinting gold, scrolled copper cups all silver chased, broken jewel-encrusted swords, and splintered chests spilling pigeon's-egg pearls. The arms of slain knights lay rusting all around. Huge cloven tracks punctured the earth, amid mounds of coin and skeletons.

She gave a low moan and sank to her knees beside one such mark. The Wizard's cup clattered from her grasp. Her flat palm and fingers fit completely within one toe of the track. Three auric-yellow hairs gleamed nearby, stiff as bristles of golden wire. One by one, the brown-garbed girl retrieved them, held them before her. They smelt of humus and burnt, bitter herbs. Hannah's hand closed tight about the golden hairs. Their odor pervaded her, gritty on her tongue. Her thudding heart shuddered, slackened, pulsed. The retreating world rolled eerily over on its side. Dank, white mist curled to enfold her as she slipped insensate to the freezing ground.

Chapter 6
Lies

"Bear! Bear!" Brown Hannah heard Magpie's cries only faintly, as in a dream. "Here. She's here!"

Yaps and barking reached her ears, bounding closer through a swirling dankness which damped all sound. The odor of foxes then, musky and warm, and small paws swarming over her, and three wet tongues lapping at her frozen cheeks, so panting hot they burned. Hannah moaned, rolled away from them. She felt stiff as deadwood, painfully numb. Snuffling beside her, and a broad paw scratching delicately at her palm.

"Hannah," wheezed Badger. "Thank the Lady we've found you. . . ." His breath scalded her. "Wake, child. Wake. You're much too cold."

The dormant girl tried to move, to speak, to lift the lids of her eyes, but nothing stirred. She felt ice in her veins, like gelid rivulets, and a great stillness settling upon her. Badger patted anxiously at her hand.

"We've brought a friend to carry you home."

Hannah gave up trying to move. So much easier just to lie motionless. A shambling presence loomed above her. She felt Magpie hopping about on her collarbone.

"Don't fear. It's just Blonde Grizzled Bear."

The foxlets licked earnestly at her temples and nose.

"Off, off! Leave her," Magpie exploded, taking wing. "Let Bear lift her."

Badger and the fox pups vanished. Hannah felt a weighty, hirsute snout exploring her side.

"You're sure she's quick?" came Bear's ponderous voice.

"Of course she's quick!" Magpie squawked. "She moaned."

A powerful paw slipped beneath the torpid girl, lifting her up. Her bones felt brittle as icicles, limbs as heavy as hailstones, her gown made of rime. She found herself lying prone on a broad surface of bearskin, the hairs all longer than her hands. Ribs and shoulder blades moved beneath the soft, coarse shag, which savored of pollen and honey and dust. The fingers of one of Hannah's hands closed reflexively about Blonde Bear's fur. The other remained clasped in a fist at her breast.

"She smells stillborn," snorted Bear, ambling to face the direction from which they had come. Hannah's weight listed.

"Hellish place," she heard Badger rumble. The foxlets whimpered.

"She's found his trove," Magpie sighed, perching atop Bear's head now, or so it seemed from the sound. "No good can follow. Let's be off."

Grizzled Bear began to walk, a gentle, rocking gait. Heat radiated from her thick, blonde pelage. Hannah nestled deeper into its warmth. Behind her the fox pups barked.

"Cup! Cup, cup, cup!"

"It's the goblet," Badger muttered. "I suppose we'd best bring that, too."

Hannah managed a feeble sound. "Lied—lied to me," she whimpered. "The Wizard lied. . . ."

Magpie chirred. "Born with a lie in his teeth, that one."

"Hurry," Badger urged. "I've never seen her so drained. The air grows frostier with every breath. We must get her to shelter, and soon."

Bear's pace increased to a shuffling slog. Hannah's awareness ebbed.

"Cold! Cold, cold—" the foxlets bayed, springing ahead through the echoing Wood.

"Wizard's work," Magpie spat. "That insatiable leech is bleeding her dry."

Little of the journey remained in Hannah's memory. She recalled Blonde Bear shouldering through the hut's narrow entryway. Warm air enveloping her, the soft give of her rush tick. Magpie flapping about, telling Bear to pull down all the spare thatch stored along the roof beams and heap it over Hannah. A delicious sense of warmth began at last to pervade her as the foxlets curled about her icy toes, Badger draped himself across her bare forearms, and Magpie settled, broody hen-fashion, beneath her chin. Bear dragged in a great mass of deadwood to build up the fire.

"She smells more lively now," Bear muttered, toward morning, snuffling her ear.

Magpie pecked gently at the brown girl's cheek. "She seems warm enough. I think she sleeps."

"I'll go then," muttered Blonde Grizzled Bear, crunching something between her teeth.

The air smelled sweet. When Hannah no longer detected that mild, nectarous scent, nor heard the grinding of massive jaws, she realized Bear had lumbered off. Dawn lay in a cold, thin line along the eastern horizon. She dozed, only fitfully aware of her surroundings. Time passed. Finally, in the late afternoon, she woke feeling battered and exhausted still, but no longer frozen to the bone.

"Pick it up!" Magpie was hissing. "Carry it."

"I can't," Badger panted through his teeth. "I'm made for digging."

Hannah stirred. From where she lay curled on her rush tick under a great covering of thatch, she beheld the kitchen of her little hut. A fist-sized poke of barleycorns, pecked open, sprawled upon the hearthstones. The tiniest pot she owned lay overturned beside a dripping ladle. Herb dust powdered the untied salt sack, which had spilled. Badger backed along, tugging doggedly at a clay cup of broth, dragging it toward her across the floor. Hannah could get no more than one elbow beneath her before her strength gave out. She rested, short of breath, until Badger reached the rush tick and maneuvered the mug within her reach.

"There," he puffed. "Can you lift it? I'd only drop it if I tried."

"So you're awake!" Magpie cawed, skimming to her from the hearth. "The savor of my cooking must have roused you."

Hannah smiled weakly at their worried glances. Carefully, exerting all her effort, Hannah grasped the cup and heaved it up beside her on the rush tick. The clay was warm, the steaming broth within thick and brown. Its aroma rose delectably. Hannah sighed with pleasure.

"Magpie," she murmured, surprised how frail her voice sounded. "I never knew you could cook on your own."

"I cook best on my own," the bird replied, preening. "I simply haven't seized the opportunity of late."

Beneath the warm, dry thatch which covered her, Hannah felt stirring and realized the fox pups still curled about her feet. Carefully, using both her hands, which shook, she brought the steaming cup to her lips. The broth was rich, mildly seasoned with thyme, its barleycorns succulent, hugely swelled. Drinking, she realized how famished she was. She had never tasted anything so delicious in all her life.

"It's wonderful, Magpie," she murmured. "A feast. But what's this?"

She spat out something small and dark, spiral in shape. The pied bird peered at the slick little shell in Hannah's hand.

"Snails," Magpie answered. "For flavor."

Hannah choked, coughing into one hand. "You know I eat no flesh. It's vile."

"They're not all vile," Magpie insisted, hopping onto Hannah's shoulder now. "Most palatable. A delicacy."

The fair-haired girl glanced sidelong at the bird. She

sipped at the aromatic broth till none remained, but she left the dozen black snail shells at the bottom of the cup.

"Eat those," Magpie urged. "Here. I'll pluck them out."

The brown-clad girl laughed helplessly as the bird ducked into the cup and brought out a snail. Using her bill, she extracted the meat, but Hannah shook her head. Magpie cocked her own.

"They shouldn't go to waste," she pronounced. Downing the morsel, she reached into the cup for another. "I've had not a bite since yestereve, and I'm famished."

Smiling, Hannah stroked her downy breast.

"What have the rest of you eaten today?" she asked.

"Butterroot," Badger answered happily, and indeed, she saw traces of the deep orange pulp between his toes.

"I sent the foxlets out chasing mice this morn," Magpie added, bolting another snail.

"What did you give Blonde Grizzled Bear for her trouble?" Hannah asked softly.

"So you remember that, do you?" Magpie returned.

"Sugar stalk," Badger answered wistfully.

"All of it?" she asked, startled.

"Both stalks."

The injured girl sighed. She had been saving two fat lengths of cane to boil into syrup. No matter, she told herself. There would be other stalks, as soon as the weather warmed. Hannah quailed to think what might have become of her if Bear and the others had not found and tended her.

"What did that conjurer do to leave you in such a case?" Magpie demanded. "Strong enough to remember is strong enough to tell us that."

"Plucked all my greenery," Hannah whispered. Memory made her skin draw into gooseflesh, her eyes well.

"You kept yourself too long from him," Badger chided.

Under her covering of thatch, Hannah felt one of the foxlets stir, lifting his head. She thought of herself lying lifeless as a frost-nipped bud on the hoof-torn earth.

"The Wizard lied to me," she hissed, gritting her teeth hard against weeping. Setting the clay cup shakily to the floor, she lay down again, hoarding her strength. "He claimed the Tanglewood hid no trove, concealed no Golden Boar, that all the knights passed safely through. But look what I stumbled on beside those heaps of arms and bones and gold."

Slowly, painfully, she opened her hand, which ached from having been clenched so long. Coarse as quills, the three stiff, golden hairs gleamed upon her palm. The pied bird peered close. Badger sneezed.

"They smell of burnt leather."

Hannah looked directly at him.

"Did you know he had a trove?"

The old brock snuffed, shook his shaggy head. With difficulty, the girl turned to Magpie, who hopped within a hand's length of her chin. The pied bird shrugged. "I thought he might. I'd never seen it."

Hannah closed her eyes, let out a deep sigh.

"It's vast," she breathed. "The Boar must be its guardian."

"Hannah," clucked Magpie sternly, "you mustn't let the Wizard know you've learned this."

The wan girl studied the three gold bristles in her grasp. "All I know of the world is his teaching," she murmured. "But I think both the Wood and this world hold far more than he'd have me know."

She stroked Badger's rough, lengthy pelt, ran one finger of her other hand gently over Magpie's cool, knobby toes. Under the thatch, she felt the fox pup sigh, lower his head, drift back into dreams. Badger and Magpie watched her. Each in turn, she met their eyes, her voice soft and steady.

"I mean to discover all."

"Enough, then!" the pied bird replied, dancing away. "You tickle me." She pecked at her own toes peevishly.

Badger kissed her hand. "We'll help, of course."

The bird nodded. "But first you must regain your strength. You're tender yet as new-sprung grass. Rest now, while I tend to supper."

Chapter 7
Mending

Hannah mended, slowly, over the next moonspan. Never before had the Wizard's draught sapped so much of her vitality. Her weakness frightened her. The weather had turned so cold that rain froze as it fell, leaving branches bowed under thin, translucent layers of ice. Frost glazed the ground. Magpie fluttered around the kitchen, knocking over pots too heavy for her to lift and preparing whatever the other beasts brought in—redbulb and water eels, carrots and cress. Those dishes the pied bird managed to complete without disaster proved surprisingly palatable, carefully seasoned with savories and spice.

Magpie, Badger, and the fox pups made good their promise to help her find out all she might of the world. Old Badger waddled down to the road to eavesdrop on cottars wending past. Magpie and the foxlets roved to the edge of the village itself, observing its denizens from as near a vantage as they dared. Hannah did what little she was able about the hut, tiring so easily still. She did not fare abroad at all for a very long time, but lay much abed, marshalling her strength.

Bit by bit, the weather did at last begin to moderate and Hannah's vigor revive, though her foliage was tardy to sprout and sluggish to grow. As her bloom gradually returned, Hannah resolved never again to allow the Wizard so great a portion of her greenery. A foreboding that should she fail to recover quickly enough, he would seek her out and demand his next infusion, regardless of her weakened state, filled her with terror. She knew she must regain as much as possible of her stamina before the turning of the moon.

"I saw a woman baking today," Magpie told her one afternoon, dropping a fresh-browned bun into her lap. "It reminded me of something. I can't think what."

Hannah stared in surprise at the perfect puff of bread nestled among the thatch. "When did you cook this?" she asked. "And from what—have we any flour?"

Magpie sat on the twigs of thatch and looked at her.

"You didn't make off with this?" Hannah exclaimed.

The pied bird fluffed her feathers. "The woman had a double dozen of them cooling on the sill. And I didn't steal it. I left her a beetle. A nice, fat one. It was shiny blue-black."

Hannah snorted, not knowing whether to laugh or chide. The bun smelled delicious. "Villagers don't eat beetles."

"Neither do you," Magpie humphed. "I'd have asked the woman if she wanted something else, had I been able to make myself understood, but those dolts don't comprehend! Now eat that. I paid a good beetle for it."

Hannah considered the bun. The gentle swell of its crust was punctured with the needle-like scorings of Magpie's toes. The baker had used white yeast, not sour leaven. Hannah could smell the clean, saltless savor. She bit into the bun. The smooth, flaky texture dissolved in her mouth. She could not stop eating until she had finished.

"I thank you, Magpie," she said at last, crawling out from under the thatch. "But promise you'll buy no more buns from the villagers. If we're to have bread, I must bake it myself."

With an effort, she rose and made her way to the hearth. Her dizziness was much less today.

"Wist! Have a care!" Magpie cried, fluttering after her. "Fall, and we can't get you back into bed ourselves. We'll have to send for Bear."

Hannah laughed weakly, sat down with a thump on the hearth. After resting, she swept up spilled barleycorns and the fragments of a shattered bowl. The fire felt wonderfully warm against her skin. Carefully, she ladled water into a hanging cook pot and swung it over the coals to heat. Badger waddled in through the entryway, a gnarled rutabaga in his jaws. Hannah thanked him, washed it, and put it in the warming water. Standing precariously for a moment, she lifted down a string of dried onions from the roof beam and added those, too, to the pot.

"I saw a cottar at his garden today," Badger panted, stretching himself out on the hearth, "scratching at the frozen earth with a stick—and don't look at me that way, Hannah. This one lay outside his plot."

Hannah sighed in exasperation, combing her fingers through the tangled mess of her bed-rumpled hair.

"Seeing him so doing, working at the soil, made me think of something," Badger murmured. "Something I can't quite recall, like a story I heard very long ago."

Hannah dropped a handful of dried peas into the broth. "Why is it," she asked Magpie and Badger both, "that neither of you recall your past?"

A moment's silence.

"I don't know," said Magpie finally. "It's like a beetle. I keep looking for it, but it's wandered off."

Badger snuffled sleepily, his ancient eyes beginning to close in the warmth of baked hearthstone.

"Do a thing for me," Hannah bade them. "Tell me whenever you half remember. And then try very hard to recall."

"I do that already," Magpie laughed. "But I'll continue."

Badger nodded, mumbled, already nearly asleep.

"The foxlets—" Hannah started.

"Foxlets!" Magpie scoffed. "They're too young even to guess their own names."

"I know," Hannah insisted gently. "And yet they were here when I awoke, that first time, that earliest time I can recall. Ask them to do the same."

❦

They had onion broth, oat cakes, and branch water that even for dinner. Hannah felt better than she had in days. She did not sleep so soundly thereafter as she had at first, in a senseless swoon. Sometimes now at night, she heard the thrashing of branches and the crashing of brush deep in the Wood. It must be the Golden Boar, she knew. That knowledge made her shiver beneath her warm mound of thatch.

When the moon turned and time arrived for her to seek the Wizard again, few shoots yet budded in her hair, and those mostly loden green hoodwink and yellow-green tattertail. Still, she did not pull them all, only those visible upon the crown. Every sprig that nestled underneath, along the nape of her neck, she let be, covering her head with a wrapping of broadcloth, as many women among the village folk did. Those few, small shoots she did pull made only a feeble broth. This she bore with trepidation to the Wizard's crossroads, deep in the Wood. He seemed disappointed, but made little fuss.

"Is this all you could manage?" he demanded glumly.

"Yes, Wizard," Hannah murmured, her eyes cast down. She spoke no further, neither of villagers, nor knights, nor of the Golden Boar. She had no wish to linger.

"A weak batch," he sniffed.

"Yes, Wizard."

He drank it off. "Well," he added, flicking the lidded cup back to her with a dour look. "It was only to be expected, I suppose, after last moon's rich crop."

"Yes, Wizard."

Scowling, he paced between the trestles, the instruments and vials. "I expect next moon's draught will be more hearty."

"Yes, Wizard."

He shrugged shortly, spun on his heel and strode away. "Well, run home, then, girl. I've work."

Mending

She left him, swiftly and without tears, relieved to be quit of her due to him for another moon. The brew that followed was indeed darker, but once again, Hannah left some of her shoots unpulled and hidden. Nor did she include in the draught every shoot she pulled. Some she set aside, that the tea might not be measurably stronger. These shoots she brewed into a separate tea, which she herself drank and felt much bolstered. Again she trekked the twisting path to the Wizard's crux, and again endured his peevish disappointment. Yet her demeanor was so meek, so quiet, he never questioned her.

Hannah carefully garnered her strength. By infinitesimal degrees, the weather continued to warm until no frost covered the morning ground. On rare occasions, the sun peeped through the high, gray overcast. Wind lost some of its chill and at times even ceased to blow. Nameless young knights still disappeared into the forest. Hannah no longer sought to stay them. None stopped or spoke or turned to look at her as they cantered the far distance, seeking the Wood and their doom.

No cottars came to her for many days. She feared her visit to their village had daunted them. But at last a few did come, and nearly a week after, a handful more, until after a time it was as it had always been—except in one regard. Now when villagers came, Hannah listened with utmost attention to every murmur that passed between them. She asked questions by way of conversation to learn more of the world beyond the Wood. Subsistence for them there was hard, she knew, much more difficult than her own. Hannah herself had always known how to forage and lay by. She had never gone truly hungry in all her life. Cottars, on the other hand, knew so little of their own environs. Most could not even tell by looking which plants were edible, which medicinal, which poisonous.

One aspect of cottars' lives puzzled Hannah above all others. That was love. She had no real notion of the meaning of the word. It seemed a kind of longing or melancholy, an ill which made the village folk miserable—yet the more they suffered from it, the more keenly they desired it. No villager ever came to Hannah to be cured of love, only to have love spurred if already it tormented them, or to become seized with love if its pangs did not yet rack them. Hannah found the affliction wholly baffling. Yet she gave them love charms whenever they asked: a forked twig, an oak gall, a twist of grass.

"Magpie," she asked the bird one noon gathering horehound and licorice along the verges of the Wood. The fox pups trotted at her heels. "What is this love the villagers all long to languish from? Is it an illness, a wandering of the wits—or some sort of sorcery?"

"Love!" the pied bird exclaimed. "I'm much too old for it."

"But did you ever suffer from it? What was it like?"

The foxlets played tag about Hannah's ankles. She had to hold her arms out for balance.

"It was like," Magpie replied, "rolling in ants and supping sweet berries at the same time." She gazed off distractedly. "It's all hazy, though. From before I came here."

Mending

Brown Hannah surveyed the tiny patch of wild, flavorsome herbs, much nipped by frost, and sighed. She had meant to glean seedlings for transplant to the herb garden beside her hut long before now, but had lacked the energy.

"So love is a rash?"

"Humph!" Magpie scratched in the dirt. Evidently not.

"Do you think Badger recalls?" Hannah pressed.

"I doubt it." Magpie snapped up an ant lion, devoured it. "Badger's older than I. It's longer ago for him."

"The foxlets?" the fair-haired girl tried hopefully. The three of them had bolted out from under her foliate skirts and sprinted pell-mell along the Wood's edge.

"They're much too young," the pied bird laughed. "Like you. Love's ahead of them yet."

Hannah looked down at the bird, surprised. "Love lies ahead of me?" she asked. "Are you saying that one day I'll suffer with love?"

"I should hope so," Magpie replied. "If you've luck enough."

Hannah could think of no reply. The notion of love seemed absurd to her. A great fuss and pother. Carefully, she pressed dirt about the roots of a seedling and set it with the others in the basket on her arm. Strange. Clearly the villagers relished their love, even as they bemoaned its pains. The fair-haired girl shrugged, smiling to herself. She doubted she would ever suffer with love. She was too unlike the villagers, surely, to share that woe. Unlike them, she had no kin, no human companions—she no longer counted the Wizard kith to her. Nor did she seem to age as the villagers did. Another peculiarity she had confirmed, with the aid of Magpie and the fox pups' spying, was that the villagers indeed grew nothing on their heads but hair: no shoots, no stalks, no buds or leaves. The Wizard had lied to her in that regard as well.

<hr />

Late one afternoon, Brown Hannah wandered the cold gray beach below the Tanglewood, digging for mussels and clams for the fox pups' dinner. The puff of cloud far to the west, beyond horizon's edge, teased at her, never quite visible, mysterious as Magpie and Badger's forgotten dreams. She always asked the fisherfolk about the towers of cloud, when from time to time she found them mending nets or caulking a leaky hull. Gruff folk, even poorer than the villagers, they spoke little.

"Is it an island?" she asked a pair this day, a father and son carefully untangling a long, fouled line. The elder nodded.

"'Tis."

"Have you ever been there?"

"Na."

Hannah shifted the little basket of shellfish on her arm. "Has anyone?" she asked.

The father shook his head, holding part of the snarl in his teeth while his weathered fingers worked the line. "'Tis a turrible place, milady."

The knot began parting. The older man held the strands wide while his son passed the other end of the line, wrapped about a spool, through the gap.

"None dare set foot there," the son added, passing his father the spool. The old man spat, unlooping the last of the snarl. The son began helping his father respool the straightened line. "Not for an 'undred year."

"Why?" Hannah asked them. Gulls cried overhead.

"Because 'tis . . . well, 'tis. . . ." The son floundered.

"Faraway, milady," the old man finished for him, tipping his cap to her in leave-taking.

Their skiff lay ten paces off. Father and son shoved it into the incoming tide, waded out and climbed aboard. Hannah watched them step the mast, unfurl the sail. The son sat amidships and bent to the oars. His father at the tiller gazed back over one shoulder at her. He pointed with his free hand.

"Yonder 'tis, milady," he called back. "Faraway!"

Chapter 8
Black Knight

The following morn dawned bleak and cold. Hannah tramped once more at oceanside. No islands teased her gaze this day, no tantalizing glimpses of a faroff shore. The dull sky hung in a seamless curtain. The woodland girl sighed. Behind her, the dark mass of the Tanglewood loomed. No sun broke through the cover of cloud. The day steeped gray as washwater and rags.

Hannah skirted barefoot beside the dunes, a cord of hemp flexed taut over one shoulder and a wide, shallow basket woven of oaken strips balanced on her hip. Here, among whispering shore oats waving, she bundled driftwood for her dinner fire, gathered beached kelp, and sorted periwinkles to crush for their purple dye. Gulls wheeled crying overhead. A sanderling herded shore fleas above the waterline.

Hannah's pale hair, combed tangleless now, teemed with the buds of irises and lilies. For the first time in nearly three moons, she felt steady on her feet again, sanguine and strong. Yet dread pricked at her. Time fast approached when she must seek the Wizard. The brown-garbed girl gazed ruefully at the unfolding shoots, most of which she would have to pull before the day was out.

"Ho, maid!"

The voice came from behind her. Brown Hannah started. Turning, she saw a young man riding along the strand. Tall and hale, he had a fine-planed face with merry, darksome eyes and sable brows. A glossy jet plume spurted from the helm slung from his saddlebow, above two boar spears strapped to his steed's black caparison. The cloak and tabard he wore over his armor were ebon as well. A silver cloakpin at one shoulder pictured a circle enclosing a leafy tree simultaneously in fruit and in flower. Its mate was evidently lost, for his other shoulder bore a simpler iron clasp.

"Fair maid," he amended, reining in as Hannah set down her basket and bundle of firewood. She stared at the knight, much more than surprised. None of the others had ever stopped before.

"Call me Brown Hannah," she answered, glancing down at her faded shift. She sighed inwardly at its many unseamed rips and frays. "None call me fair. Why do you speak to me at all?" she asked on a sudden, glancing up. "Your fellows never did."

The young man smiled, a flash of teeth all even and white. Hannah felt her skin flush. He was even handsomer than the others had been, those fledgling knights who had passed before. Lost now, every one, to the Golden Boar. How many dozens? Hannah's heart ached. The young man's black hair lifted in the cool, salt wind. This one must be the kith of foxes, thought the brown-garbed girl, to have such a foxy grin. Not Ruddy Fox, nor his cousin, Gray—but Swart Fox, darker than ravens' wings.

"Then the more fool, they," the other told her, affably, "to pass by so comely a maid with never a word."

Hannah's blush deepened, for comely surely she was not. Unless he meant the flowers in her hair. Perhaps that was it. Now that they had begun to grow in such profusion, she felt far less lifeless and drab. Belatedly, she opened her mouth to make reply, but the young man was already speaking.

"I seek a treasure, Brown Hannah. A miraculous thing, stolen long ago. It lies hidden now, transformed or disguised. Have you heard of such a marvel?"

"I've heard tales," Hannah told him, "though I know them to be false. Marvels are for holyfolk, and miracles for children's rhymes."

"Nonetheless," pressed the knight, leaning forward. "I entreat you, tell me what you've heard."

Hannah looked away. Her pulsebeat quickened uncomfortably. She did not want to send him to his death. A dune snake slithered past her skirt. Low waves foamed, rippling along the shore. The flat sea spread like a leaden tablecloth, falling beyond horizon's edge. Above, robber gulls fought over scraps of fish.

"Cottars whisper that the treasure's a damsel," Hannah murmured. "That the treasure's a tree. Or a beast fantastical. But it's none of these!" She turned to face him once again. "Nothing but dross heaped up at the heart of the Wood."

"A wood?" the young man exclaimed. "One deep and impenetrable, known as the Tanglewood?" At Hannah's nod, his eyes caught fire. "Such is the Wood I seek! Can you tell me where it lies?"

What use? Hannah thought. What profit to mislead him? If she did not tell him, some other surely would. Still, she shivered in the cold, thin ocean wind.

"There," she answered, nodded to the inky, silent trees bordering the strand, gnarled branches fingering the air. "But hear me," she bade urgently. "The trove you hunt can't be seized—a sentinel jealous and terrible stands guard." She glanced once more at the shadowy Wood. "Venture in, and the Golden Boar will kill you sure."

The young knight only laughed, very reckless and high of heart. His dark cloak snapped in the rising breeze. The metal of the bitpiece pinged and chinked. The stirrups of his saddle creaked. The boar spears nodded as his mount champed and bridled, impatient to be gone.

"You're a fool," Hannah told the horse.

"What choice have I?" the taut white stallion snorted, hooves churning the sand. "He rides me. I bear him. I must go where he bids."

"You could plant your hooves, or feign a limp, or pitch him off and run away, taking his spears with you," Hannah snapped. "Who is he, in any case? Where's he from?"

The horse tremored the skin of his shoulders in a shrug and tossed his head. "I've no idea," he answered tersely. "He only bought me five days back. I don't know where he's from."

The knight did not seem to hear their words—just as the cottars and the fisherfolk, who likewise paid her no heed whenever she conversed with animals. Hands on hips, the

girl glared at the young man's charger, but the great beast
only sidled, rolling his eyes.

"Carthorse!" Hannah hissed at him. "You'll kill your
rider and yourself as well. Spit out that bit, dunderpate.
Nag!"

The stallion whickered and laid back his ears, but the
young man only turned his mount's head with the reins.

"Lend me a kiss to be my shield," he laughed. She
dropped her hands and looked up at him, startled. Gaily dar-
ing, his black eyes met hers. "When I return, Hannah, I
pledge to pay it back to you."

Wind thrummed through the nodding oats, rustling her
gown. Hannah felt no mirth, only pressing sorrow. She
pulled her unruly locks back from her face. The petals of
nearly all the buds had begun to open. Fear crowded into
her thoughts. The Wizard would be expecting her. Quickly,
she shoved panic aside, still facing the young man square.
She shook her head.

"No man returns from the Tanglewood," she told him
sadly. "No shield lies in a kiss."

The white steed ramped, strained toward the Wood.
Hannah bowed her head and fell back to let him pass.

"Wait!" she cried the next instant, whirling to catch the
rein.

The warhorse whickered and would have reared, but the
young man checked him, held him shuddering. The mewl-
ing cries of gulls overhead seemed muted, unnaturally
stilled. The sea had ruffled now, whitecaps spinning across
its rills. Hannah gazed up at the black-haired knight. He sat
staring down at her, no longer laughing. She stepped closer

to him. He leaned, cupping her elbow in one hand, and lifted her up. She stood with one foot in his stirrup, her bare sole pressed to the cold metal of his solleret. Trembling, the white horse stood perfectly still.

"Take this instead," she said, easing a pale lily from her hair and pinning it with a thorn to the young man's breast.

Why had she done that? Hannah wondered. What better shield might a lily prove than a kiss?

Sighing, she sprang down and turned away, left the young man-at-arms fingering her bloom in surprise. Bending, she caught up her driftwood cord, retrieved her basket of periwinkles and kelp. The knight called to her as she trudged away. He called again, but she did not turn. What hope? she thought bitterly, setting her teeth. The boar would end him like all the rest. A hummingbird spiraled lazily about the nectar-laden cloud of her hair. She waved it off and slipped a new stick into her bundle. When she heard the other's horse wheel and spur toward the Wood, saltwater spattered her drying kelp. She pretended it was only ocean spray.

Rain fell in a fine, desultory mist. Brown Hannah fussed about the rush hut. The weather had warmed enough that she had rebundled all her spare thatch and piled it back among the roofbeams. Despite the dense, muggy air, her kelp had shriveled into nearly nothing. She kindled driftwood on the coals and put a kettle on to boil, stirring in the kelp shreds to make jelly. But swatting at robber flies, she forgot to watch the pot, and the whole thing scorched into a stinking mess, which she had to throw out into the yard. Hannah sat on the hearthstone, biting her lip and scrubbing the kettle out with moss.

"You're lovestruck," laughed Magpie from a beam overhead.

"Surly bird," Hannah snapped. She sighed heavily.

"I used to sigh just so during my courting days," wheezed Old Badger, waddling near.

Hannah glared at him, and hung the kettle up. The song of bees droning in her ears was driving her to distraction. One by one, very gently, she pulled blossoms from her hair: snowwhite dune lilies and purple irises, swamp pinks and yellowflags, salmon-colored dwarf day lilies and pale blue gentian trumps. She sat looking at the heap of them in her lap. Never before had her locks yielded such rich bounty. Though she knew she should fling them onto the midden, they were far too fair to cast away. She set them in a bucket of branch water, but they withered within the hour.

"Pity," Magpie clucked, picking at one. "They reminded me of something. I can't think what."

"I saw such things as these once," Badger sighed, chewing meditatively at one crumpled stem. "I'm sure of it. If I could but recollect where."

The woodland girl ground her teeth. Where might that have been? she brooded bitterly. The stark Tanglewood itself harbored never a flower. Why could none of them remember anything of their past?

"Meddlesome pother!" Hannah burst out, upending the birchbark basket that had held her periwinkles and finding it empty. "Hermit crabs, every one, and all strayed. And where's the sea lettuce?" She could not find it. "Now nothing's left to steam the turnips with but saltroot and vinegar."

Evening drew on. Hannah found sprigs of hemlock and bitters, wormwood and rue growing upon her crown. She yanked them out angrily and threw them onto the midden. Her head ached. Supper had no taste. Later, Hannah tossed fitfully atop her rush tick. Her dreams were all of knights breasting foaming waves, setting sail from a strand overseen by pale, cloud-topped cliffs. She woke at moonset. The misting drizzle had ceased. Cool steam hung in the night air without. Howlets hooting within the Wood sounded like dying horses' cries. Hannah rolled, jostling the foxlets curled at the foot of her bed. They roused, grousing. She stroked them till they settled, then lay back down herself, dozing. Flowers opened before her in dreams. First light woke her with a start.

"Perhaps the young knight on whom I pinned my lily has not yet met the boar," she found herself murmuring. "With luck I might still warn him away . . . !"

"Where off?" her bedfellows barked after her. "Where to?"

Hannah paid them no heed as she ducked out through the rush hut's door and hastened full-tilt through the dawn haze into the Wood.

⟡

Brown Hannah sped through the tangled trees. Their bare, bony branches seined the morning light. She cast about her for signs of passage—turned stones, broken twigs, the ashes of a camp. But she found nothing. No birds called. No creatures crossed her path. The Wood stood cavernous, still. The odor of boneset and lavender, cure leaf and healer's herb wafted from her hair. The nape of her neck itched with trickles of sweat. Her bare feet made no sound on the cool, damp earth.

Morning wore away. Hannah sank down upon a boulder to rest. A murmur of water reached her ears. Rising to follow it, she came presently to a shallow ford. A black-plumed helm lay dented in midstream. Clear current spilled through the visor, then on between the fist-sized stones upon which it rested. Deep ruts as from pivoting hooves cut the mud of the bank. Two boar spears, unbloodied, lay trampled nearby. The tall steed in black caparison sprawled lifeless at the water's edge, his injured rider in the saddle still, held fast by one leg.

"I'm too late!" gasped Hannah, running to him. "He met the Boar yesterday. . . ."

She knelt beside him on the rocky bank. The young man shuddered, too weak to do more than stir in his heavy armor. Sticky darkness matted his hair at one temple. A line of desiccated blood strayed from one nostril to his chin. His lips were cracked, dry. Hannah cupped her hands to the cool stream chuckling beyond his grasp and held them to his mouth. He choked, drank, staring up at her, too faint and feverish to speak. Her lily, white and unwithered, still bloomed upon his breast.

Hannah unclasped first the fine silver cloakpin shaped like a tree, then the makeshift iron brooch. She parted the seams of his tabard with his hunting knife, then reached beneath to unbuckle his armor, each piece weighty as an iron kettle. Feeling with care along his linen undertunic, she found no more bleeding, only bruises and one cracked rib. Satisfied, she used his greave to dig in the slick, stony mud under the horse's side. The young man swooned before she had finished. His leg was broken at the thigh.

"Leave him," hissed Rain Crow from a branch overhead. "Can't you see he's done for?"

"I won't," muttered Hannah, shoving clay and pebbles to one side. "This one's mine. You can have the horse."

"Horseflesh," Rain Crow cackled, hopping along the limb.

Hannah threw a stone at him. "Fly and fetch Blonde Grizzled Bear," she ordered.

Rain Crow flapped sullenly away. Hannah dug and rested, rested and dug. The young man twitched but never woke. She brought him more water after a time. It was noon before Blonde Bear lumbered out of the trees, her brassy fur smeared with honey and crumbled wax. Hannah had cleared the earth from about the fallen rider's leg, but she needed Bear to drag him free. Hannah unbuckled the last of his armor: the kneepiece of his injured leg. Rain Crow watched from across the stream.

"Whew!" said Bear, snuffling the young man curiously. "He smells of foxes. Foxes and sorcery. Who is he?"

The brown-clad girl shook her head. She did not know. Binding his leg with splints of broken boar spear, she steadied him on Blonde Bear's massy shoulders. When they finally reached her hut, Hannah laid the young man on her hearth and built the fire up roaring to stop his shivering. She washed his face and daubed the blood from his hair. Then she gave Bear a great spoonful of jam for her trouble and sent her off, licking her snout and growling with pleasure. As Hannah sat pulling willow slips from her coif to bruise into a poultice, the young man roused.

"The Boar," he muttered, shuddering. "Red eyes burning and cheeks all flecked with slaver. Slew my horse, but wouldn't touch me. Saw your lily and drew back, squealing with rage." Weakly, the young man clutched her arm.

"Be easy," murmured Hannah, crushing the green slips to make them ooze. "You're safe. The boar won't find you here. What's your name?"

Panting, he shook his head. "None who serve . . . my Queen may know his name . . . till he accomplish the quest."

"None accomplish it. It's impossible," Hannah snorted, wrapping the bruised willow in a scrap of cloth and pressing it to his brow. "Who is this Queen?"

The young knight's eyelids drifted shut. Ever so faintly, he smiled. "Faraway. . . . She fostered me. . . . A thief stole her treasure long ago. Countless of her champions . . . have sought to reclaim it." His smile slipped, voice growing bitter. Painfully, he turned away. "Now I, too, have failed . . . and shall never know my name."

"Peace," Hannah told him, smoothing the poultice down. "I must call you something. While you bide with me, your name shall be Prince Foxkith."

He slipped at last into a quieter doze. His fever fallen, he would sleep till nightfall. Hannah took the withered flowers from the day before and dashed steaming water over them. The resulting tea was weak and pale. She poured it into the

Wizard's rune-carved, lidded goblet and swathed her hair in a coarse woolen cloth, the lush profusion of her remaining greenery bundled unseen underneath. She no longer needed to steal sips from the Wizard's covered cup to strengthen herself. Hoarding her hair's yield and harboring as much of it as possible to flower unplucked gave her more stamina than she had ever before known. Feeding the fire again and bidding Badger keep watch, she lifted the brimming goblet from the hearth and hurried from the hut.

Chapter 9
Foxkith

The Wizard was not in his lair. The place was dark and still, the bare ground clammy but not nearly so cold as it had been before. The humid air had warmed. Hannah waited expectantly, shifting from foot to foot, gaze darting amid the shadows and the swirling fog, but the Wizard did not appear. At last, fearing to leave her wounded guest untended any longer, she left the covered goblet with the Wizard's watered dram standing atop his trestle board, among his geared instruments of copper and brass, the uses of which, he had boasted once, were the study of stars and navigation at sea. Hastening homeward through the Tanglewood, she heard far-off concussions, as of falling limbs or upturned trees. A horrible, hoarse keening like the bawling of swine drifted on the windless air. Hannah fled away from it. It did not follow, eventually faded as she neared the verges of the Wood.

As she emerged from the trees where the hut should be, Hannah stopped dead. A great mass of thorns had sprung up about the edge of the yard, taller far than the reach of her arms. It was much too dense to see through, with long, wicked spines. From where she stood, mouth agape, she could barely glimpse the roof of her rush hut beyond the wall of briars. A moment later, Magpie skimmed over the thicket's top to land at Hannah's feet.

"Magpie!" the girl exclaimed. "What is it?"

The pied bird twitched her long, ribbonlike tail. "Thorn hedge," she answered flatly. "What does it look like?" Magpie fluttered into the air to alight on Hannah's wrist. "Didn't used to be there," she clucked. "Now it is."

"But how?" the woodland girl exclaimed, extending her hand so that Magpie might hop the length of her arm to perch on her shoulder. "How did it come to be?"

The pied bird shrugged. "Baffles me," she said, plucking the corner of Hannah's headwrap till the girl pulled the whole thing free and shook her head to let her fragrant locks breathe. The warm sapor of flowers permeated the air. Magpie teased a nettle at the nape of Hannah's neck. "One of your thorns must have fallen," she muttered. "It's all I can think."

"But what I pull always withers," Hannah murmured, then in afterthought, "save for Foxkith's lily. . . ."

Slowly, she approached, holding one hand out to test the thorns. But the branches shrank from her, parting to let her pass. The brown-garbed girl stepped through, stood on the other side of the briars now, within their compass, which circled the whole yard. Turning, Hannah saw the spines merging once more to seal the breach.

"There!" Magpie cried in triumph, pulling free a soft, green thorn from Hannah's hair. Gingerly, she let it fall, and as Hannah watched, the slender spicule twitched, turned, and burrowed into the soil. Young tendrils twined upward to join with others of the hedge. The greenwood girl stood speechless, stared. "As I thought," Magpie chirped. "Badger and the fox pups can all wriggle through. I fly over. For you, they part. They must be your making."

Dusk was drawing on. The high hedge cast the yard into deep shadow. Hannah could think of no reply. Awe left her able to move only slowly. No charm of such power had ever sprung from her before. No green thing from her crown had ever taken root elsewhere and flourished. The wonder of it both astonished and delighted her. Magpie laughed.

"I don't know how your young knight will fare," she began, "when he's well enough to attempt to pass through."

A low groan sounded from within the hut. Whirling, Hannah caught her breath. "He wakes!"

Magpie took wing. As the leafy-haired girl disappeared through the open doorway, the pied bird called after, "And I doubt those thorns will yield to any Golden Boar!"

<hr />

Foxkith's leg took two moons to mend, his first days flat abed, plastered with poultices to cool fever and ease the pain of knitting bone. In addition to the teas she brewed him from the healing herbs crowding among her hair, Hannah fed him grilled shoots and greens, peeled roots, steamed bulbs and birds' eggs, churned butter and milk the one-horned neat had lent. He took it all gratefully.

She herself drank only water, of course, and never

touched animal fare—but she knew, as she had always known, exactly what her black-haired knight needed in order to heal. In time, when his head grew clear, Hannah fashioned him crutches from the shafts of his broken boar spears. Thereafter he hobbled about gamely, chafing to be hale. The days continued fair and mild, and as Foxkith's need for herbs grew less, her hair produced fewer and fewer of them until it gradually became a profusion solely of fragrant florescence.

"What lovely tresses you have, Hannah," he told her one morn, as she stood with a supple leaf unfurling amid the silken, straw-colored strands wrapped about one finger. Before he spoke, she had been nibbling the green point, lost in thought. "I've never seen the like."

Laughing, Hannah plucked her twigs and savories to crush into powders, cure, crumble, or concoct. Oddly, ever since the thorn fence grew, Hannah had begun discovering charms she had never known before. One day, as though she had always possessed the knack, she changed three smooth riverstones into radishes simply by smoothing them between her hands. Though she had always been able to kindle fire, soon she learned that if she cleared her mind and concentrated hard, she could boil water without bothering to light the fire. No one taught her such tricks. Urges simply seized her. Soon she began trying any notion that wandered into her head, just to see what it might yield.

"Best not let the Wizard see you at that," Magpie warned the day she turned a freshwater clam into a butterfly.

Such trifles of conjuring delighted Hannah and impressed Foxkith no end. He himself had no talent at all in the sorcerous arts, though Hannah patiently demonstrated, trying to teach him every new skill she discovered. But he could only throw up his hands, laughing, all fingers and thumbs. He could not even summon a broom by whistling. Hannah was at a loss to explain his lack of ability, for Blonde Bear had said he smelled of sorcery. Indeed he did: a clean, pungent savor like fresh basil.

And Hannah herself began to smell of sorcery. It arose from within her somehow, from her very blood. Now when cottars came, they goggled awestruck at the high thorn fence which parted to let the flower-haired healwoman through. She always bade Foxkith bide within, fearful that if villagers learned she harbored a wounded knight, news might somehow reach the Wizard or, worse yet, his Boar. Often at night now, beyond the tall barrier of thorn, she heard the great swine crashing and squealing in the Wood. The healing knight never seemed to wake, sleeping easy all night upon the hearth.

Once more at the turning of the moon, while Foxkith slumbered, Hannah trekked in secret to the darkwood's crux with her verdant hair tightly bound under woolen cloth. Once more, she found no wizard awaiting and so, after an hour, having scant wish to linger, she left the tepid, watery draught, and returned another day to retrieve the lidded cup. She told Foxkith nothing of the Wizard or of her visits to his lair at the Tanglewood's heart.

Instead, as soon as he grew sound enough, she asked him to speak of himself and his quest. His last few months, he remembered well enough: traveling on foot along the seaside roads, searching for news of a fabulous treasure; working piecemeal here and there for board and a place to sleep; apprenticing himself to an armorer long enough to fashion his armor and weapons; acquiring his horse for a pittance from a grateful burgher whose two young sons he had pulled from a burning shed. It was only when she asked after his Queen that Foxkith's memory grew uncertain.

"I cannot remember her, Hannah," he told her earnestly one evening as they sat upon the hearth twisting hemp into a cord. "Only that she's wise and kind and sad, without child of her own." He smiled slightly, gazing directly at her as he was wont to do. "Like you, Hannah," he added quietly. "You remind me of her in some strange way. I can't think how."

Hannah felt her cheeks redden. That Foxkith's past remained as mysterious to her as Magpie's and Badger's, the fox pups' and her own frustrated her no end. She bowed her head to fuss with one of the tiny twin spindles in her lap.

"So your Queen raises nameless fosterlings instead," she murmured, trying to tease more out of him without seeming to, "on a far-off isle . . . ?"

She had been reluctant at first to press him, but as weeks had passed and he grew more able, she began to suspect it was neither fever nor her remedies which clouded his memory.

"Faraway," he echoed, nodding.

"And each spring, a fresh troupe of your lady's newmade knights set forth," Hannah continued, allowing two fine-spun strands of hemp to twine together, "vowing not to return till her stolen treasure be found and restored?"

Deftly, he reached to straighten the forming cord as it threatened to knot. All his movements were skillful and sure. The touch of his hands on hers made Hannah's breathing deepen. She swallowed, glanced away. The young man seized the tail end of the hempen cord, began to loop it onto a shuttle. The fair-haired girl watched the firelight play across the smooth hearthstones.

"Whoever eventually succeeds upon this quest is to be rewarded with his name?"

Foxkith shrugged apologetically. "It's all I can recall."

Hannah let out another arm's length of the two twisted strands she held, allowing them to merge into more cord for him to wrap. "Why is that?" she asked. "Why would your Queen dispatch so many without clear memory? Is she a sorcerer?"

The young man looked off a moment, frowning. She studied the fine, illumined edges of his profile. "Yes," he said at last, dubiously. "I think she is."

Hannah leaned back, maintaining proper tension on the cord. She eyed him a moment longer. Still he gazed off, lost in thought. She tried to keep all bitterness from her voice.

"Why do you think she robs you of your wits before sending you. . . ." To your deaths, she wanted to say, but managed at the last moment to amend it: "On such a fearful quest?"

The young knight lost his hold on the shuttle of twine. It skittered away from him. She saw him wince as, without thinking, he shifted his weight to reach after it. Sweat broke across his forehead and upper lip. His hand went to the splint at his thigh.

"There, leave it," Hannah told him hastily, stepped on the cord to keep it from unraveling.

Old Badger roused himself and waddled over from the

rush tick to pick the shuttle up in his teeth. He stood on toes to offer it back to Foxkith, who took it with a murmur of thanks.

The young knight sat a moment not looking at her, his breath coming harder as he rewound the cord.

"Will you have a slip of willow?" Hannah asked, reaching to her hair.

He shook his head, managed a smile. "No. It's easing. But Hannah," he told her, "I don't think my Queen purposely takes our memories. I think it's . . ." He cast about. "I think it comes from the fate that we, as her knights, choose and . . . because of the . . . change. . . ."

"Change?" Hannah asked him. "What change is that?"

He frowned again, searching. "I don't know. A . . . change."

She looked at him and could find no deception there, only puzzlement. "You trust her then, this Sorcerer Queen, despite the deadly task she lays upon you, and this change?"

"With my life!" Foxkith exclaimed. His eyes sought hers.

"Ho," Magpie laughed from the roof beam. "And all of you pay with it; that's sure."

Hannah shook her head, dismayed. "You think this missing treasure's worth your life?"

The young knight smiled ruefully. "The treasure," he answered, "whatever it may be, matters nothing to me in and of itself. I search for it only because of its value to my Queen."

Hannah thought of the vast, useless cache at the center of the Wood—mere wealth and arms, that offered neither sup nor haven nor fellowship—and could see no sense or purpose to it.

"What good is this treasure—what worth?" Her words were the barest whisper, but the young man caught them.

"To my Queen, everything, more than her life. . . ."

"Than the lives of her fosterlings, you mean," she retorted angrily—then found herself instantly sorry. It was too late to unsay it now.

Taking no offense, Foxkith shook his head. "We're volunteers, Hannah," he said gently, "every one among us. No one compels us to undertake this quest."

Hannah's eyelids pricked at the thought of so many youths devoured by the Boar. Blinking, she studied the twine forming in her lap, both spindles nearly empty now. "Why doesn't your Sorcerer Queen come herself to claim her treasure and face the Boar?"

"She can't leave the isle," Foxkith responded, without hesitation.

Hannah looked up at him. "Why's that?"

His eyes, so clear the moment before, clouded then, his dark brows furrowing, as though the answer eluded him only barely. "I can't say," he conceded at last. "It's her destiny, I think—or her doom. Just as it's her knights' to seek the treasure."

He said nothing for a little space, winding the shuttle. Hannah made twine. At length, he spoke.

"You've dwelt in these parts all of your life, Hannah. Daily you venture the Wood. Have you never glimpsed this thing, my lady's hoard? For wherever it lies—however disguised—I must find it."

The brown-garbed girl bit her tongue. She had come to the end of both hempen strands. Carefully, she twined them into the final length of cord, allowed Prince Foxkith to roll it up. She dared not look at him when next she spoke. "I've seen nothing," she lied. "Nothing at all." Then, truthfully: "No treasure worth dying for awaits you at the heart of the Wood."

Chapter 10
Lovestruck

After that, Brown Hannah vowed never to speak with Foxkith of his failed quest or his Sorcerer Queen, lest he make foolish vows and brood on what might have been. Instead, she did her utmost to divert him from such bootless thoughts. She set him to scrubbing kettles and sweeping the hearth. Happy to be of service, he proved handy enough, planing boards to fashion a new tabletop and restore the missing cupboard door. He mended all her worn willow baskets, patched pots, and sharpened cutlery. The herb jar he shaped from river clay fired strong and solid as a brick, and from a cast-off horseshoe, he forged fishhooks, a door latch, and seven new iron nails. The foxlets doted on him.

"Cousin?" they asked, though he plainly did not understand their speech. "Smell like us."

"He's a useful enough lad," Magpie chattered, stealing a sweet pea from Hannah's hair. "Small wonder you cavil to give him up. Face it, girl. You're lovestruck."

Hannah sighed, sorting springbeans for supper. Afternoon sun streamed in the door. Foxkith sat at hearthside across the room, laughing with the ruddy young foxes, seizing them by their scruffs and wrestling with them. They barked and shouted at him, nipping his hands. On the mantel above him rested the Wizard's closed cup. Hannah had steeped a feeble brew earlier in the day. She knew she must bear it to her master that evening, while the young knight slept. Magpie pecked at her fragrant, crinkled flower.

"Next time, the Golden Boar will make mincemeat of him."

"I know that very well," Hannah murmured. "And so does he. Yet it doesn't seem to matter to him one whit. There's no reasoning with him. His wretched Queen's doing, by her sorcery. I wish I might keep him safe here, forever."

Under the table, Old Badger wheezed with merriment. Hannah blushed. She knew the young man's welfare was but half the reason she had prolonged his convalescence with such care, ever counseling patience and urging him to forebear, put no weight upon his injured leg until it was well and thoroughly healed. Yet the more she brooded, the more she realized how lost she herself would feel when time came at last for Foxkith to depart. In all her uncounted years within the Tanglewood, Hannah had never known close human company before. She found she liked it very well.

"When the prince's leg is mended, you must decide," Badger said, crawling into her lap and scattering the beans. "Keep him prisoner, or set him free to seek his fate."

Hannah nodded glumly. The thought of losing Foxkith bit at her heart.

"Lovestruck!" cawed Magpie, skimming away through the open door.

The young foxes followed, tumbling out into the sunny yard in a flurry of snowy throats and russet pelts and mincing, coal-dipped paws. Foxkith laughed and let them go, one crutch leaning against the hearth. The other he laid across his lap and took his hunting knife to, whittling one end into a point.

"What are you doing?" asked Hannah, leaving Badger to the scattered beans and going to the knight. Foxkith set aside the knife and stake.

"My leg's mended, Hannah," he said, taking her hand and pulling her down to sit beside him on the hearth. "It bears my weight now, if painfully. Soon that, too, will pass, and I must seek the Boar."

Hannah stared at him.

"Without horse or arms?" she exclaimed.

His battledress lay rotting by the riverside, hard by the bones of his murdered steed. She had imagined that upon mending, he might be made to see reason, persuaded to abandon his quest, fare forth into the world instead and return no more. Or if not that, at least urged to replenish his weaponry. She had never heard tell of any armorers nearabouts. That alone might keep him gone for moons—and much might happen in those moons. Another knight might preceed Foxkith's return and succeed in killing the Boar. The Boar might depart of his own accord, or die of age. Something, anything . . . ! She had never once suspected Prince Foxkith meant to venture again so soon into the Tanglewood. The young man kissed first her one hand, and then the other.

"I swore my Queen I'd find her treasure."

"Then you swore to perish!" the healer girl exclaimed.

He shrugged stubbornly. "I must win a name for myself, Hannah."

"You have a name," cried she. "The name I gave you!"

He looked at her, but did not answer. There was no moving him, she saw. Poised there, her hands in his, she could have wept. If this pain I feel is love, Hannah thought, then I wouldn't seek it for all the world, nor wish it on another. . . . Yet, now that she suffered its hold, she wanted never to be parted from it—though she realized with both certainty and dread that to spare his life, she must part with Foxkith now, this day. For the sun might darken and the world might end before she would send him to the Boar.

"Very well," she whispered hastily, squeezing his hands. "Your heart is set, I see. I'll help you on your quest. But mark me: no treasure lies within this Wood. A savage Boar, yes—but he guards nothing. That rumor's just a ruse to draw your Queen's knights from the real trove, which lies far north of here. I've . . . I've often heard the cottars speak of it."

It was untrue, of course. But she knew of no other way to save him. Telltale nettles and tendrils of nightshade crept nascent from her temples and behind her ears to twine together at the nape of her neck. She dared not touch them, tug at them, lest he know she lied. Instead, she gazed up at him, desperately willing him to believe.

The young man sat looking back at her, his black eyes perplexed. "Why haven't you told me this before?"

"Forgive my deception," she breathed, meaning every word. "I wanted to keep you . . . here with me. I've never shared my roof with a human companion before. I . . . joyed in your company."

Nervously, Hannah pulled free of him and fetched the shawl she used now when carrying the Wizard his draught. She lapped it snugly about her head, hiding her blooms and briers from view.

"When I return, I'll tell you the road and give you provisions for your journey." She seized the covered cup from the mantel stone, aware that she was chattering. "But first I must take this tea to . . . to another I tend. The need is very urgent. I mustn't delay."

The brown-garbed girl turned, but Foxkith caught her gently about the waist.

"A moment, I beseech you," he said. "Who's this invalid to whom you bear the cup? Twice before you've filled it and ventured forth by night. Why is that?"

Hannah's eyes widened. She had never realized Foxkith had noted her absences. Fear stole through her. "No one. A cottar. No one of consequence," she stammered. "I won't be long. Sharpen your spears."

He let her go. She fled the hut, clutching the tepid cup to her breast. She felt the young man's gaze following her across the yard, was grateful after passing through the wall of thorns to hear them merging, impassable, behind her, locking Prince Foxkith inside, safe from the tusks of the Golden Boar and the murderous schemes of his Sorcerer Queen.

The Wizard was nowhere to be found. Hannah stared about her at the empty spot, inhabited only by his movables and vials. She set down the cup and retreated, anxious to rejoin Foxkith and divert him from his reckless course. She knew she ought to hurry, to fare straight home—and yet, inexplicably, she found her steps drawn to the Wizard's treasure. She had no trouble at all finding it. Her feet guided themselves. It lay within a mere stone's throw of the Wizard's lair. What surprised her most was that in all her years in the Tanglewood, she had not stumbled upon it sooner. The brown-clad girl stood staring, she knew not how long, at the vast, glittering expanse of coin and jewels among the rusting shapes of cast-off armor, the remnants of bleached bone.

"Hannah!"

Foxkith's hale echoed through the Wood like a horn. Hannah whirled, taken by surprise, heart beating like a captured bird. The young man stumbled from the gloom, the stakes that had once been his crutches—and before that, spears—grasped for walking staves in either hand. He limped badly, his expression furiously vexed. A moment later, Hannah saw what impeded his gait: not the soreness of a new-mended leg, but Badger. The old brock had sunk his teeth into the other's heel and, splay-pawed, was dragging like a deadweight.

"We tried to hold him," Badger wheezed.

Exasperated, Foxkith prodded the shaggy creature with the blunt end of one stave until his furry assailant released the shoe. The fox pups, panting and yipping, seethed about the young man's legs. He forged through them, plowing toward Hannah like a drowning man thrashing to shore. She saw in alarm that his forehead and cheeks, throat, wrists and hands bore dozens of scratches, some deep, though the white lily pinned to his breast remained fresh and unscathed as the day she had placed it there.

"Cut his way through the thorns with the kindling axe!" Magpie screeched, swooping to seize a hank of the black knight's hair. She back-winged furiously, as would a moth caught in a cobweb. Foxkith winced, ignored her. The foxlets began to howl.

"Be still!" Hannah gasped. "Magpie, release him. He's here now, and nothing any of us do can change that."

The fox pups sat and stopped their crying. Badger left off trying to seize the other shoe. Magpie spat out the young man's lock and fluttered to the ground, much ruffled, her tail feathers askew. Foxkith stood panting, leaning on his stakes, staring at the heaps upon heaps of precious things beyond the fair-haired girl. His face shone bloody and bleak, no trace of elation there. Hannah pulled the shawl from her head and moved to daub an oozing weal on one cheek. He let her. When she had done, he reached into his jerkin. Withdrawing his hand, he extended it toward Hannah, palm up. There lay the three golden hairs which until now, she had kept hidden on the shelf, concealed beneath the Wizard's cup.

"He found them on the mantel after you left," Badger murmured, cleaning the dirt from his claws.

Foxkith did not seem to hear him. His gaze found Hannah's.

"Is this treasure yours, Hannah?" he asked her softly, nodding all around. "Are you some sorceress? Is the Golden Boar your beast?" The three hairs glinted on his palm. His black eyes seemed infinitely saddened, his voice astonished with pain. "Are you the thief who stole my lady's trove?"

Hannah stared at him. "No!" she whispered, reaching to clutch his arm. "It all belongs to the Wizard. The Boar's his, must be. And the treasure."

"What did you carry in the cup?"

"The draught I must bring him at each turning of the moon."

"Why?"

The Wood was very still. Hannah let go his arm. She gazed at him, baffled. No words came to her. At last, helplessly, she shook her head. "I don't know. He commands it— has always commanded it. I . . . cannot say why."

A pause. The young man's gaze appraised her. "Why didn't you tell me where the treasure lay?"

"To keep you from it," she answered. "To keep you safe."

He weighed her words. "You meant to send me far from here."

She nodded. "Yes. That you might live." Her voice grew ragged. Tears threatened. "Either way, I had to give you up. I couldn't spare myself losing you. I hoped at least to spare you your own death!"

All at once his countenance softened. The golden hairs fell from his hand. He drew closer, touched her hair. "From the first moment I saw you, I've loved you, Hannah." His words were low, no more than a whisper. "I could never give you up. When I've accomplished my quest and go from this Wood, come with me."

Now tears did fall, salty on her lips.

"Your Sorcerer Queen has sent you on a fool's errand," she told him, shaking. "The Golden Boar can't be defeated. All who undertake to do so perish. . . ."

Prince Foxkith laughed softly, as though she spoke non-sense. "Kiss me, Hannah, and I won't perish."

His fingers brushed her chin. Very gently, he put his mouth to hers. She tasted ocean tang and the bite of metal, the steaming sweat of horses and the musk of foxes, a sweet savor like the nectar of dune lilies, and a smoky attar as of sorcery.

"O Hannah," the young man breathed, "you taste of green things growing."

Chapter 11

Golden Boar

All at once, Hannah heard a cracking and a crashing all around, as of timber falling and underbrush upturned. Magpie flew into the vaulted space above the trove screaming, "All this billing and love-smacking has brought the Boar! Did you think it wouldn't?"

Old Badger melted into the earth in a storm of dirt and churning claws. The young foxes scattered into the Wood. Hannah whirled. Not twenty paces from her, a huge razor-backed beast shimmered darkly in the gloom, coarse bristles gleaming, stiff as golden filament. His ruby eyes glistened. His ivory tusks gnashed. Great hooves, like axeblades, broke the bones where he trod. The Wizard's covered flagon stood, upright and unspilled, clenched between the massive ivory cusps.

Brown Hannah shrank back, still clasping Foxkith's hand. "Flee," she whispered, swallowed. "I'll draw his eye."

Already the young man was hefting his whittled stakes. He squeezed her fingers. "Stay here, Hannah."

He strode forward, past her, before she could stay him.

"So, Boar," called Foxkith, tossing his black hair out of his eyes, "will you surrender my lady's trove?"

Treasure heaps shifted and trembled as the Golden Boar ramped, stamping the ground till it shook and tearing up clumps of soil with his long, curving tusks. Magpie flew at him with a shriek, but he only gnashed and ducked his head. Foxkith balanced his lance.

"Don't think you can put me in fear of you." His voice was steady. "I've Hannah's kiss to guard me now."

Before him, the Golden Boar bellowed and shouldered a thicket of budding blackthorn to splinters. Hannah stood transfixed, staring at the Boar, at the coal-red carbuncles of his eyes, at his yellow teeth, at the Wizard's cup, at the molten glimmer of his pelt like burning gold. Her gaze fell to the three wiry hairs at her feet, the bristles exactly matching the monstrous Boar's shag. Why had she never noticed before how precisely they resembled the whiskers of the Wizard's beard? Anger and astonishment flooded her. With a cry, Hannah dashed past Foxkith to plant herself between him and the Boar.

"Hannah!" the young man burst out. "Stand aside—"

"I won't," she answered stoutly. Then, turning to face the Boar: "Wizard, wear your human shape."

Abruptly, the Golden Boar ceased his ramping, then with an angry peal, began to seethe and shiver. The air about him wafted hot. The Boar's image wavered like candleflame. In another instant, he vanished, and the Wizard stood before

them, garbed in cloth-of-gold crusted with garnets and carbuncles, his rune-inscribed flagon gripped in his hands.
Foxkith stared. The Wizard glared back. To Hannah, the
older man looked drawn and worn, the thinnest she had
ever seen. She poised between him and the young knight
still.

"So you've kissed him, girl," the Wizard growled. "Better
to have left him to the Crow."

"Hannah, who's this?" the young man behind her
breathed.

"The Wizard," she managed. "The Wizard of this Wood."

"What are you to him?"

"Nevermind what she is," the Wizard spat. "She's mine."

Hannah felt Foxkith's hand slip into hers.

"You're her father, then?" the young knight asked.

"He's not," Hannah hissed. "I've none. None that I
know."

The Wizard laughed. "Of course I'm her father." His
beadlike eyes flicked back to Hannah. "I raised you, didn't I?"

Foxkith's hand fast about hers gave her courage. "Magpie and Badger raised me," Hannah exclaimed. "I raised myself!"

The Wizard smiled a thin, tight smile. Brittle laughter escaped his lips. He snapped his fingers. Red sparks flew. A
white cabbage moth flickering past became a pearl, which
dropped with a thump into his palm. Still smiling, he spat on
it, polished it against his sleeve.

"I'm your creator, Hannah, even if I'm not your sire. I
conjured you, just as I did this stone, from nothing, out of
the air."

Hannah pressed her lips together. Her face grew hot. She was no village lout, to be bandied so. "Call me no conjurling," she countered tersely. "Nothing comes of nothing. I must have started somewhere. Badger and Magpie say they half remember a place, another home. . . ."

The Wizard's eyes flashed, hand clenched about the cup. "They lie!" He changed the pearl into a hazelnut and crushed it. "I created them as well. No place ever existed, for any of you, before this wood."

"Not so!" the fair-haired girl protested. "That can't be." Though she did not yet fully understand every facet of the other's deception, the puzzle was growing clearer by the heartbeat—and with it, her heartsick feeling of betrayal. "It's you, you who lie. You who've lied to me—"

"What of it?" the other snarled. Wordless rage rumbled in his throat. Hannah recoiled as his finger stabbed at her across the air. "Moon after moon have I languished," he thundered, "awaiting a draught worth downing."

He toyed with the lid of the cup, gazed contemptuously at its contents.

"Instead you've dallied, mending this rover's limb and letting him guzzle what's rightfully mine—that he might attack me anew. You little wanton! Look what's come of your neglect. Now your hair's in flower, and all my Wood, and your gown grown green."

Startled, Hannah stared, realizing for the first time that her robe had indeed lost its shabby hue. Verdant as new leaves, it draped now in delicate, translucent layers. Jasmine and honeysuckle bloomed about the treeboles all around their heady savor pervading the glade. The tangled boughs overhead were budded in leaf. Sunlight beyond shone stronger. The air held a strange freshness, a wild, clean feel. Hannah herself felt giddy, brimful. Taken unawares, she gaped. Preoccupied with Foxkith, she had noted none of it before. Bumblebees droned lazily about her fragrant crown. The young knight lifted her fingers to his lips.

"Bear up, Hannah," he murmured. "You're no more conjurling than I. Trust nothing this magicker says."

"Silence, you meddlesome cur," the Wizard grated.

Hannah gathered herself. "Who owns these riches?" she demanded. "Were they plundered from Prince Foxkith's Sorcerer Queen?"

The Wizard snorted, his tone become at once exasperated and conciliatory. "Child, child . . ."

"I'm not your child!" the fair-haired girl threw back. "You'd no more hand in my rearing than . . ." She cast about. "Than the bones of these hapless young men."

To her surprise, the other burst into laughter. Then he hawked derisively. "They were hardly men, my dollikin. Look more closely at what lies at your feet."

The confidence of his tone chilled her. Hannah stood a moment uncertainly. Slowly, she peered down. The dimness thickened, shifted, thinned. Fleeting sunlight fingered through it. All at once, she saw that what scattered the damp leaf mold were not human bones at all, but the relics of wild wolves and civets, martens and stags. She heard Foxkith draw sudden breath. A shudder seized her. She fell back staring. Yet the greaves and cuisses, breastplates and gauntlets that lay scattered among the broken skeletons were all of manly shape. Beside her, Foxkith fell to his knees, staring at the wreckage, incredulous, sifting through it, lifting to examine now this fragment, now that.

"Animal bones," he whispered. "The bones of beasts . . ."

She heard the Wizard's short, harking laugh. "Your comrades, dog." His bloodshot eyes sought Hannah. "Now listen, wench. This lickspittle's mistress keeps no human company. Once, long past, I visited her isle—but fled in disgust. Now she transforms her brutes into men-at-arms to seek me out and harry me."

On his knees, Foxkith ran his hands through the clattering bones, his voice a windless whisper still. "Beasts . . ."

The Wizard glanced at the young man, a thin, tight smile twisting his lips. He leaned toward Hannah, his voice urgent.

"Pay no attention to that sweet-tongued little stray. The crone he serves is monstrous. Malformed. Inhuman."

Hannah could think of no reply. Horror welled in her breast. Turning to stare at the older man, she wondered how any queen, however sorcerous, could prove more foul than a massive boar which savored human flesh. Her revulsion must have shown upon her face. Across from her, the Wizard sidled.

"I kept this from you to . . . to spare you," he sputtered.

Hannah watched the dappled light playing across the carbuncles that patterned the yoke and placard of his goldstitched gown. His claim's absurdity astonished her, infuriated her. She could not have fashioned an answer had she tried. The other's brow quirked. His lips pursed. Her unwavering gaze seemed to disconcert him. His eyes darted away. For a moment, the pointed, upturned toes of his silk slippers absorbed his whole attention. Beside her, she felt Prince Foxkith start.

"Animals, animals," he muttered, then suddenly exclaimed, "That's it! I remember now." He turned, face exultant, dark eyes shining with urgency. "Hannah, I recall! I know what my Queen—"

"Stop your barking!" the Wizard exploded, so suddenly that Hannah jumped.

Foxkith sprang to his feet, eyes now locked on the older man's. "Did you think I wouldn't puzzle it out?" he demanded. "Never recognize you for what you are?"

Hannah's eyes flicked to Foxkith.

"Not another whimper," the Wizard growled. "You've wildered my chattel quite enough."

The young man's expression had hardened into hatred. "I know you," he said quietly, "and I know your deeds. Hannah, he's—"

"Hold your tongue!" the old man roared, drowning the other's words.

Foxkith had turned to her, lips parted for speech. Savagely, the Wizard made a clenching gesture. Hannah felt the sudden buzz of power in the air. The young knight's eyes widened. He gasped. Bits of bones tumbled from his grip. One hand went to his throat. His chest heaved, lips working silently. No sound issued from him but a rush of voiceless air. Hannah stood rooted. Foxkith's eyes found hers. Consternation blazoned his face, mirroring her own. The green-garbed girl reached out to him. Across from them, still cradling the cup, the Wizard chuckled mockingly.

"There. That's as it ought to be."

"What have you done?" Hannah cried.

The other chortled. "Just stilled his baying. It wearied me."

"Release him!" Hannah found herself shouting, more angry than she had ever been in her life. "Release his voice."

Foxkith spun once more to face the Wizard, his own mien one of pure outrage. Catching up one whittled shaft, he hefted it. The older man ignored him, eyes still on the green-garbed girl.

"Would you see what your pet knight was before his sorceress gave him human shape?"

Foxkith stood with one arm cocked, poised to launch his shaft as, swifter than a striking snake, the Wizard tore a carbuncle from his own samite robe and hurled the jewel at the silent young man. Hannah cried out, too late. The stone struck the knight squarely on the temple and burst in a puff of roseate smoke. Foxkith staggered. Reddish haze enveloped him. Both wooden shafts toppled, useless, from his hands. His knees buckled, his half-obscured form shrinking, wavering. The miasma thickened, roiling about him as he fell to earth. A moment later, it dispersed, and what lay on the ground was no longer a man but a fox, black as burnt sugar, with a splash of white fur like a lily on his breast.

"Foxkith!"

Hannah ran to him. The swart fox struggled up and stood swaying, one hind leg bearing his weight only gingerly. Bloody scratches covered him. With desperate haste, Hannah ran her hands through his thick, jet-black pelt, but could feel no injury save for the thorn cuts and his tender leg. He stared about him dazedly, lost his footing, lurched upright again. Not a sound escaped him.

"You see?" the Wizard crowed. Hannah heard his footsteps crunching toward her across the bones. "He was a fox! An enchantress's hound, nothing more."

The boar spears clattered away across the bones as the Wizard kicked them violently. Between her palms, the mute fox shuddered and shrank. She felt as though she, too, had been vanquished with a single stroke. The Wizard's breath behind her was a rasp. Bent double, upon her knees, Hannah could not bring herself to look at him. Burying her face in the dark fox's fur, she wept.

"Little fool," he hissed, bending over her. "You should thank your luck. I'd have killed him, too, like all the rest, if your ward hadn't still been pinned upon his heart."

Chapter 12
Thorns

Hannah whirled to stare at him. The Wizard recoiled, stood panting before her, out of words. A nervous wince pinched his cheek. His gaze darted warily about. Self-consciously, he cleared his throat, interlaced his fidgeting fingers about the cup. Foxkith slipped from Hannah's grasp and crept a few yards off, limping. Still choked with tears, she gazed hard at the thin old man in the samite robe.

"Why must you kill them?" she demanded, hating him.

Suddenly, the other could not look at her.

"Any knights I spared would only have returned," he muttered.

Sweat beaded his brow. His colors seemed diminished, less bright than they had been only a scant while before. He appeared drained. The fair-haired girl said nothing. Her sobs were subsiding now. The Wizard twitched. She watched him swallow dryly, tongue tip stealing across his lips. Abruptly, he turned.

"Enough chat, girl. I thirst. Where's my draught?"

He lifted the lid of the rune-carven goblet still clutched in his hand, peered briefly into its depths, then with a snarl of disgust, cast it to the ground. Its contents trickled among the bones. Hannah saw the black fox cringe. She caught no glimpse of any of her other companions—Badger hidden in the earth, Magpie flown, and the ruddy fox pups retreated into the trees. She faced the Wizard alone.

"And I want a true draught, this time," he growled, "well-steeped and darkly brewed. The last half-dozen you brought were little more than water."

Noon sun peered through the budding branches of the Tanglewood, brighter than Hannah had ever seen it shine. The clearing stood filled with golden air mingled with shadow. All around her, the Wizard's riches glittered. Wiping the tears from her cheeks, she left the wooden goblet lying on the ground and walked to a great, spilling chest of gems. Deeply absorbed, not looking at him, she nudged a square-cut topaz with one toe.

"Did you steal all these from the Sorcerer Queen?" she asked him softly.

The Wizard grunted, began to pace. Stooping, he plunged one hand into a mass of silver pence. The coins slipped shining through his fingers. They showered like hail. With a smirk, the Wizard straightened, moved on, stooped again, stirring this heap and that with anxious, grasping hands.

"These? Hardly!" His smile broadened. "I took far more than mere riches from that misshapen monstress."

Watching him, Hannah thought how she would like to bury him in his own coin. Still the Wizard paced. A chuckle. A nod.

"How little you know of the world, my chit. Outside this Wood, nobles and villeins use tokens such as these for pittance. For barter."

"I know of barter," Hannah answered evenly.

The other seemed not to hear. His hands played over the glistening hoard.

"*Steal* this—from that island hag? Never! All this is mine, come to me by way of tribute."

"Tribute?" the green-garbed girl murmured, startled. She knew she had heard the word before. A moment later, its meaning dawned. "From penniless cottars!" she spat.

The Wizard's laugh grated against the stillness. Sunlight glanced across the carbuncles patterning the back and shoulders of his gown.

"From cottars, yes. And kings. Seeking to buy what I wouldn't surrender for all the ransom in the world. . . ."

Hannah stared dry-eyed at the hoard all around. Her tears had vanished as abruptly as they had come. His refusal, even now, to admit to the theft filled her with outrage. She felt newfound courage welling up, pervading her, growing stronger with every breath.

"Were their lives worth this treasure?" she whispered, lifting her eyes at last. "Their misery this gold?"

The Wizard halted, staring at her. "Be still now," he commanded. "Brew my draught."

Hannah locked her gaze with his. "Foxkith told me his Queen lost something." So angry she could scarcely speak, the green-garbed girl chose her words with care. "A thing more dear to her than life itself."

The Wizard's palms scrubbed against his sleeves, his expression suddenly haunted. "You speak of matters that don't concern you. . . ."

The fair-haired girl looked at him. His lies sickened her.

"Why do her knights come here," she countered quietly, "if not for this hoard?"

"Silence!" The other set his teeth, livid with rage. Yet for all his fury, he looked weary, spent and ill. Hannah felt her own ire quickening to match his. She folded her arms.

"If the gold isn't the prize the Queen's retainers seek, what draws them to the Tanglewood?"

The old man's eyes looked to her like those of a beast caught in a snare. "I'm no thief. . . ."

Hannah would not let him go. "Oh, no? Then what has set those young knights against you?"

"Ingrate," the Wizard hissed. "You're nothing but my cupbearer. How dare you question me?"

"How dare you lie?" Hannah demanded. "How dare you steal? How dare you kill! I should have questioned you before now."

The Wizard's eyes narrowed into slits. "Time was you served me sharp and never tarried," he muttered. "Now all you do is quibble. And after all of my tender care."

The flower-haired girl compressed her lips. She had known more tenderness with Foxkith these last three moons than ever she had from the Wizard in years upon years.

Unexpectedly, he smiled, his tone growing smug. "Tend the beldame's whelp if you must, minx. See how much comfort he is to you now." An ugly laugh. "But soon or late, I think, you'll hunger for human company again—and then you'll come to me."

Hannah's anger sparked.

"You're less human than the beasts of any sorceress-made men," she flung at him. "What are you but ravening beast?" She snatched the overturned cup from the litter of bones and cast it back at him. "Brew your own draught," she shouted. "I'd sooner keep faith with a fox."

The wooden cup's edge struck the Wizard's lip, drawing blood. With a bellowing cry, he dashed it aside. It crackled into flame at his touch and vanished in a sparkling shower. Hannah felt the waft of heat, heard the snorting grunt. The pupils of his red-rimmed eyes dilated. His outline blurred, melting. His whole being began to shimmer.

"You worthless drudge, I'll drub you within an inch of your life," he wheezed. "I'll pull every shoot from your crown and shut you away in your thorn-walled midden for all eternity."

With a rolling ripple like air from an oven door, he became a great golden boar again, trampling the undergrowth, thrusting saplings and chests of booty aside. Gasping, Hannah stumbled back. The monster reared before her. His breath burned the air. Treasure melted in its heat. When his forehooves struck the ground, the earth jolted beneath the shock of heels heavy as hammer blows. The boar was charging. Hannah fell back with a scream, cornered against a great heap of coin.

Like a raven darting at a snake, the dark fox that had been Prince Foxkith sprang past her to bury his teeth in the ear of the onrushing boar. Heaving and bellowing, the aurous beast pitched to a halt. The mute fox held on, scrambling as the Boar slung his head from side to side. Yapping and snarling, russet foxlets flashed from the trees to add their teeth. Badger erupted from the ground in a shower of stones and soil. Magpie stooped like an arrow.

"False, faithless wretch!" she shrieked. "Petty conjurer!"

The Boar ducked, lunging first at one attacker, then another. Hannah scrambled after the whittled stakes that had been Foxkith's boar spears. As her hands closed over the first shaft, the wood burst into thorn. Whirling, she cast the sharpened pole with all her might. It sailed inexpertly, struck the ground two feet short of the mark. The spiny shaft stood vibrating. Roots swarmed into the ground. Thorny tendrils sprouted, reaching toward the Boar. Hannah heaved the other, greenly teeming lance. It struck to one side, instantly rooting.

The furious girl rushed closer, tearing rosepricks and greenbriers from her locks. As she flung these after the pair of spears, their spines rooted and intertwined, rising into a thicket which closed over the massive, struggling Boar and his half dozen, far slighter adversaries. Tighter and tighter the thorny spicules pressed, until the golden beast lay pinned on his side, unable to stir. Foxkith, nimble as a hare, slipped free, trotted limping to Hannah's feet and sat there licking his sharp, white teeth. Badger and the red foxes slithered after. Magpie perched on top of the briers, pecking down at the huge swine. The Boar shuddered, flickered, and became a wizard once more. Blood trickled from his wounded ear.

"Hannah," he moaned, so much more pinched and spent than the green girl had ever seen him that she stood dumbfounded. "Release me," he gasped. "I'll do no harm."

Chuckling, Old Badger shook the earth from his pelt. The fox pups crept near, grinning and wagging their heads.

Slowly, Hannah approached, careful not to draw too near. Watching her, the other's bleary eyes rolled.

"Have you ever spoken a true word?" she breathed.

He squirmed. "Give me the draught."

"Restore Prince Foxkith to human shape."

The Wizard's gaze grew hopeful. He hesitated, panting, seemed to wrestle with himself. Then softly, "The draught first? You wouldn't begrudge me that?"

Hannah said nothing, fingering the profusion of flowers opening among the silken, straw-colored strands of her crown—the ones he had threatened to again wrest forcibly from her scant moments before. She found mistletoe growing among the blooms. How she loathed him.

"You begrudged me my freedom," she answered flatly, "brought harm to me and to those I hold dear."

"No, child!" the Wizard pleaded, struggling feebly. "I could never harm you. . . ."

Hannah touched her scalp, still tender—even now—from his harsh plucking, moons ago. Fear warred with hatred in her breast. She shook her head, incredulous at his brazenness. "Speak no lies for once," she bade him. "Admit that you stole from Foxkith's Queen—"

The Wizard made an inarticulate growl, lashing out with surprising strength. Thorns rattled and nettles quaked.

Magpie flew, calling, "Be off! Who knows how long your thorns can hold?"

Hannah fell back one measured step as her adversary strained toward her. Shaking, she refused to run. He subsided finally, panting, pale. The green-garbed girl studied him, appalled.

"You haven't the power, have you?" she whispered at last. "You've spent the last of your magical stores, and without my draught, you haven't strength enough to change him back—or free yourself."

The Wizard's breath was a sob. "Don't you see?" he cried. "I'm dying. Without the draught, I'm ruined. Undone. . . ."

Hannah hardly heard him. She gazed down at the black fox at her feet. Uncertainty fled. When she spoke, it was half to herself and not at all to him.

"I must find Foxkith's Queen," she said quietly, "somewhere in the world. Surely she can restore him."

Bending, she lifted Badger; the fat old brock nestled in her arms.

"No, Hannah!" the Wizard shouted, beating desperately at the clinging thorns. "Don't desert me. I reared you from a little slip. I've been nursemaid and guardian and playfellow to you. I'm all you have in the world. . . ."

"Magpie was nursemaid to me. Badger my guardian. The fox pups my playfellows."

Hannah clenched her teeth, trying to make her voice hard. Despite herself, the words caught in her throat. Her eyes welled up again. A desperate longing consumed her, to know her history, her fate, herself. She studied the brilliant green, translucent tissue of her gown, so strange still to her eye. What lay beneath? She had no notion. She had worn this odd garment all her life. The filmy layers seemed to go on forever, as impenetrable as the mystery of her own memory. She had no recall of times far past. How often had cottar women come to her with suckling babes, tots teething or toddling? Yet she could retrieve no such scenes from her own experience, no bustling aunts or dandling nans. No sibs. No mother's arms.

The Wizard writhed. "Don't leave me. Daughter, the world's a cruel place."

She felt no pity for him. What pity had ever he shown her, or the cottars, or the knights? Anger nearly throttled her. "Claim no kinship with me, Wizard," she told him fiercely. "I'm none of yours."

A great pain, like a millstone, lay across her heart. If she stayed longer, she feared it might begin to bear down, crushing her beneath its terrible weight. The green-clad girl bit her lip to keep from groaning aloud. The Wizard called after her as she turned away.

"Come back! You won't survive. The world beyond, it's barren: death! Safety lies here. Here alone! My treasure—"

The other's hoarse cries turned to shrieks as the nettles snagged him. Terror rose in her, hearing his predictions—or were they curses? Was any of what he said the truth? Unable to stop her tears, Hannah broke into a run. What awaited her? She had no notion, even as she rushed blindly to discover it. But surely, once free of this terrible place, she would be able to collect her wits and remember who she was and whence she came and whither she strove. Laughing and yapping, the red foxes coursed after her. Badger nuzzled her cheek. Mute Foxkith loped foremost, spearheading their flight from the Tanglewood, while Magpie skimmed above, screaming.

"High time! How many years did we languish in that conjurer's thrall? We should have quit his beastly Wood long since."

Chapter 13
Green Hannah

Green Hannah fled from the Tanglewood, across barren meadows and blasted heaths. Scarcely a reed or a blade of grass grew anywhere. Hardly a treelimb bore a bud or a leaf. Through her tears, her vision seemed to change somehow. No longer encompassed by the enchanted wood, she could discern great distances without the slightest effort. Yet all she beheld was desolation, scarcely leavened by a bloom or a speck of green. No one crossed her path. She saw only a few folk far off, scratching about their flimsy huts. Their clothes were ragged, their lank frames rawboned. Strangers, all of them. No one she recognized. Their gaunt faces haunted her. Hannah ran on.

Everywhere she passed, shoots and blossoms showered from her hair. Warm breezes wafted around her. Gentle rains fell, followed by calm, fair skies. A nimbus—strangely luminous and at first roseate, then viridescent, next meline, now heliotrope—shifted and swirled about her and her companions as they sped, coupled with the odd, ineffable sensation of traveling a furlong, a bowshot at every stride. Her feet scarcely touched the earth. The setting sun and rising moon interchanged, became a blur. Far in the distance, the Wizard's wild ranting receded to a dull, cavernous rumble, at long last fading away.

Hannah ran till she could run no more. Gasping, she sank to her knees in a stony clearing halfway up a sparsely treed slope. She had no idea where she was. It seemed to be morning, by the freshness of the air, and she remembered glimpsing the waning moon. So she must have run through the night—or perhaps, many nights. Uplands loomed above her. The ground beneath her was hard and bare. She sat, more weeping than winded, while Magpie paced her shoulder and clucked. Sleepy Badger snoozed in her lap. Red fox pups swarmed tussling about her knees, and black Foxkith licked her tears.

"He said I'll die," Green Hannah panted. "The world's to be my death. . . ."

"Who? Who?" the foxlets yapped.

"The Wizard?" Badger snorted. "What a liar!"

Trembling, Hannah shook her head. "Everything's barren."

"Well," Magpie said firmly, "you don't look dead to me."

Hugging the fat old brock, the green-garbed girl considered.

"Where am I?" she said at last, drying her tears on one gossamer flag of her verdant gown. "Foxkith, where should I go?"

The black fox did not answer, only stood on tiptoe, braced two neat forepaws against her collarbone, and nuzzled her ear. Hannah turned to their companions.

"What ails him?" she whispered, then to Foxkith. "Don't you know me?"

"Don't know," the red foxes answered, snapping at one another's chins and tails.

"He doesn't speak our tongue," cawed Magpie. "Never spoke it. A man at heart."

"Well, he speaks nothing now," Old Badger yawned. "The Wizard's stilling of his voice remains in force."

"But can he reck my words?" Hannah asked, running her hands through the dark fox's thick, downy pelt.

"Who can say?" Magpie chattered, worrying a stalk in Hannah's hair till the white florets sprinkled down like blown feathers. "When first he came to you, he was already half-sensical. Likely your Wizard's meddling's finished the job."

"Peace!" the green-clad girl exclaimed, batting at the falling petals and shooing Magpie away. "In time, perhaps his memory will clear. . . ." The millstone of terror and grief again bore down upon her breast. She drew deep breath to force it back. "As it seemed to do just before the Wizard silenced him," she finished steadily. "But how am I ever to find his Sorcerer Queen if I can't even bid him to lead me to her?"

"Maybe he's forgotten the way entirely," Magpie observed, chasing after a glass snake, "along with all notion of himself."

Hannah had to bite her lip to keep panic from swallowing her. Foxkith's case was sorrow enough. What of her own memoryless state? She had told herself when she had fled that surely her own missing memories must soon return—yet she felt no closer to them now than she ever had while imprisoned in the Wizard's Wood. Her mind was a roil of apprehension. Foxkith was not the only one among them in need of sorcerous aid. How she longed to have him back in human shape, for the sound of his voice, the strength of his arm, his steady mien and air of boundless confidence. Badger padded her arm gently with one broad, flat paw.

"We'll discover a way to restore him," he promised. "Never fear."

Hannah wiped her cheeks again, exasperated with herself. Weeping accomplished nothing at all. With difficulty, she found herself managing a smile. Foxkith had paid no attention to their exchange. A spring leaper landing on the grass near him caught his eye, and he dived after it. Hannah reached to stay him, but he jumped, nipped her lightly, and slipped through her fingers, bounding after the hopping thing.

Hannah pursed her lips, shifted, then started, catching her breath. She sat among grass—grass where none had been growing only moments before. Gazing, she saw the whole stony space about her peppered in newsprung blades. Violets and tiny primroses threaded up between the stones. Foxkith crouched now, a few paces before her, gazing back down the hillside in the direction they had just come. Heath and moorlands stretched to the horizon. The runaway girl heaved a great sigh of relief to have put the Tanglewood so far behind her. Thunder's far-off grumbling disquieted the air.

Yet cascading down the hillside from where she sat and fetching across the land like an ever-widening road lay a swath of green freely specked with blues and yellows, pinks, purples, and red. Hannah could only stare at this meandering greensward wending the barren land—for surely it must be the route she had taken in her flight. Yet the trackless way she had so blindly hastened had been leafless, fallow. Now, even as she watched, the verdant strip below was widening, gradually spreading like a river overflowing its banks.

Hannah shook her head. Blossoms and leafbuds rained all around. She saw them take root where they fell. Had such sprigs from her hair done the same all along her path, springing up, fanning behind her as she fled? Hannah rose. Lost in grief, never casting a backward glance, she had remained until this moment completely insensible to the trees bursting into foliage, fields teeming suddenly into flower. Hannah held out her hands to the distant verdure, crying out in delight, "What is it? What is it?"

"It's you, dear one," the black-and-white bird answered, alighting on the green girl's shoulder with a fat katydid clamped struggling in her bill. She glumped it down. "Here's what you've been meant to do all your life, it seems."

"What your greedy Wizard was draining out of you," Badger amended, "for his own foul use." The fox pups frolicked about, yapping. The fair-haired girl sank down again.

"I'd no idea," she murmured. "I never dreamed . . ."

"Seems there's more to you than any of us dreamed," Magpie remarked. "Perhaps Foxkith's sorcerous Queen can explain these marvels." The pied bird took wing. "Meanwhile, if you can green this land, those mangy cottars and the flea-bitten wildlife you love so well needn't suffer so hard a case."

As Foxkith strayed near, Hannah reached out, seized him gently by the scruff. He rolled, mock-biting and kicking at her hand, then sprang up and darted from her.

"If I can achieve such things as this unawares," she called, "surely I can find your far-off Queen and see you made a man again!"

The fox pups sported tumbling after Foxkith, now streaking up the slope. Magpie flew graceful, long-tailed above. Hannah lifted old Badger, his gray-wealed head already nodding.

"Simply ask along the way, sweet," he murmured, drowsily. "Some beast or other's bound to have heard of this sorceress."

Green Hannah laughed, flowers falling from her hair. "So I will," she promised, climbing after the others. "Foxkith, lead on!" she cried as the swart fox hurtled away up the hill like a black and shooting star.

They traveled uplands now, looking out over flat moorlands planing down to a distant sea. She had come far north of the Tanglewood, she realized, many miles inland. The terrain here was hillier, more woody and less lush, its vegetation a darker green. Hannah steered them clear of human folk, ever mindful of how she had frightened the cottars that day in the village. But of every bird or beast she met—some of whom she healed—she inquired after the Sorcerer Queen. Fieldmice playing among knotted roots, draft mules pastured in a field, honey-brown bats flitting by moonlight—none had heard of such a one. None knew the road to her lair. None proved able to converse with Foxkith, who remained distractable as a half-grown cat.

Green Hannah

Hannah trekked on. Sometimes she found her sleep disturbed by troubling dreams: the imprisoned Wizard berating her, commanding her to abandon her quest. Yet the dawning of each successive day found her more easily able to keep doubt in one small, wayward corner of her mind and fare on, determined. No disaster overtook them, and wherever she went, the greening followed. Shoots and leaves, falling from her hair, took root everywhere. Air warmed, its balmy breezes gentling. The sun grew kinder and more often visible. Insects sang through the night, droning hums and bell-like chirping sweeter than birdsong. Food abounded. The animals Hannah encountered and questioned were no longer thin and meager, but sleek and hale. Fewer and fewer needed her healing arts.

As days slipped into weeks, Badger dug for roots and bulbs. Magpie found stalks and salad greens. The fox pups fished for mussels and crayfish, and Foxkith brought coney and dove to the supper fire, though Hannah herself never partook. In time, she crossed through country that was no longer dormant, already green. But though the fair-haired girl thrilled to the land's burgeoning and the lifting of hardship from its inhabitants, she felt no nearer finding the answer to the riddle of Foxkith's transformation than she had the day she had left the Tanglewood.

Now, standing shank-deep in a marshy place sprung with cattails and bulrushes, Hannah sighed. Badger wandered along the bank, turning over stones to look for grubs. The fox pups dug at the water's edge, while Foxkith rustled unseen through the reeds nearby. Magpie perched on her shoulder as the green girl stood cooling her feet. The sun shone positively warm. Hannah had felt thirsty upon first entering the pool, but now as her leaf-colored gown absorbed the clear, cool water, the fair-haired girl felt strangely satisfied, her thirst quenched.

"None of the beasts know where she's to be found, Magpie."

"Young Foxkith's Sorcerer Queen?" The girl nodded. The pied bird shrugged. "Small wonder," she chirped. "Sorcerers are human folk. Why should beasts trouble themselves to learn conjurers' whereabouts?"

Once more Hannah sighed. She waded deeper, parting the reeds, searching for Foxkith. "Then I must ask human folk."

Magpie bobbed. "So it seems."

The dark fox had vanished. The green girl moved further into the reeds in the direction of greatest commotion.

"But the cottar folk fear me," she murmured. "Before I went to their village, I thought it was the Wood they feared. Now I see it was me all along, because of the Wizard and the Boar."

"You've come far from that village and the Wood," Magpie mused, digging her toes into Hannah's shoulder to keep her perch against the waving rushes as the girl forged steadily through. "None hereabouts would know such things."

Hannah shook her head. "They'll know I'm not one of them," she answered. "Once, I was plain enough almost to pass for a cottar, but now?"

She gazed at the vivid green of her tissue-thin, many-layered gown, touched the fair mane that hung down her back, as lush with greenery and blooms as a garden trellis. Magpie clucked.

"Cover them," she suggested. "Both gown and hair."

Beyond the last stand of rushes, Hannah glimpsed open water, another portion of the bank, heard splashing and laughter. Peering from among the tall green cattails, she beheld five girls, little younger than she, gathering up laundry that had been spread to dry atop the bushes near the bank. They wore only shifts. Two chased each other gleefully through the shallows, slinging water at one another. Another knelt at the waterside, pounding a leather apron with a stone. The other two folded linens before laying them in two great, handled baskets. One of these last dragged from the bushes a ragged cloak stitched from odd fragments of cloth.

"Leave 't!" her companion exclaimed. "The old beggar that cast 't off didn't even want 't."

The other paused uncertainly. "Mam said we was to wash 't and see how 't came out."

"Well, now we see," the first girl scoffed, reaching for a linen tablecloth to fold. "Dingy old thing."

"Nay!" the other cried. "'Twas gay once. Look at all the colors. Just faded like."

The cloak was indeed a patchwork of many hues, all bled and paled to a subtle mingling of nondescript colors. The first girl reached past her companion to drag a nightshirt from the bush.

"Probably crawling with vermin," she muttered.

"'Tisn't!" her comrade huffed. "'Tis perfectly clean. I washed 't myself."

"I meant the beggar."

The girl with the cloak subsided. "Why'd he leave 't behind, d'you think?"

Their two companions sporting in the water dashed past.

"Didn't need 't anymore!" one called.

"Too hot for him."

"'Tis spring! Spring!"

At that, the two on the bank each cast away what she was holding and leapt to give chase.

"Look! I'm the Spring Maid," one of them shouted, holding a couple of cattails upright against her ears. "The Maiden of the Spring."

Her companions chased after her in high hilarity, trying to catch the grassy reeds out of her hands. Hannah, still among the rushes, turned to Magpie, perching quietly upon her shoulder.

"What does she mean?" the green-haired girl asked.

One of the pursuers succeeded in wresting a cattail away from the forerunner. Magpie ruffled.

"How should I know? Maybe this wellspring's enchanted."

Her companion considered this. The cottars who dwelt about the Tanglewood were ever regaling one another with tales of nymphs and sylphs and selkies. Hannah herself had never seen one.

"You think this Spring Maid is some water sprite?"

The bird shrugged. "As likely an explanation as any."

Hannah glanced about a trifle uneasily, not the least bit eager to encounter magical persons other than Foxkith's Sorcerer Queen. Before her, through the rushes, the four girls raced to and fro, spray flying everywhere till the fifth— older than the rest—rose, wringing the sopping apron, and called, "Enough. All of you, back to folding. If we're late to table, there'll be none left."

Giggling, the four shirkers abandoned their reeds, crowded out of the water and set to folding the last of the laundry with a will. The shabby cloak lay forgotten where it had fallen.

"Spring's also a season, I think," Magpie chirped.

Hannah frowned. The word meant nothing to her. "A season?" she asked.

The pied bird laughed. "Yes. It's when the weather changes."

Again Hannah shook her head. "But the weather never changes. It's always cold and drab. . . ."

She stopped herself, for she realized what had once been the unalterable sameness of weather no longer held true.

"Oh, it's changed right fair since the Wizard stopped draining you," Magpie laughed. "Spring, spring. I haven't seen it since—since before I came to the Tanglewood. When was that? I can't recall. My mind's as muddled as your Foxkith's. . . ."

Done wringing the apron, the eldest girl directed two of the others to seize the first, full basket and begin lugging it up a path leading from the pool. The other two laid the last of the folded linens in the second basket and made to follow. Draping the damp apron over one shoulder, the eldest took a last look along the bank as though scanning for any garment they might have been missed. Her eye fell on the abandoned cloak. She hesitated, then shook her head and turned away. Without a thought, Hannah stepped from the reeds.

"Wait!" she called. "Won't you take the cloak?"

The first two girls with their basket had already disappeared around a bend, but the second pair and the eldest girl paused, turning to look behind. Hannah waded toward them. The three remaining girls stared, eyes wide, mouths open. Reaching the bank, Hannah bent to lift the cloak and held it out, took a few steps in the direction of the motionless trio.

"You didn't mean to leave this, did you?"

One of the girls holding the basket screamed, a high strangled sound. An instant later, her companion joined her. Their basket dropped heavily and lay on its side as the pair dashed screeching around the turn of the path and away. Astonished, Hannah stopped in her tracks. The last girl stood rigid, shaking. She thrust out both arms as though to keep the green stranger at bay.

"No harm, Maiden. No harm," she stammered. "Keep the cloak and welcome. We didn't know 'twas your pool! We've washed here all our lives—"

At that, fear seemed to overwhelm her. She spun and bolted up the path after the others, whose cries still sounded. Foxkith bounded out of the reeds and skipped up the path, halting to sniff at the overturned basket. Hannah whistled.

"Hist, Foxkith. Leave it! That isn't ours."

Quick as a deer, the shadow-colored fox sprang up and shot back into the reeds in the direction of Badger and the others. Hannah stood dismayed, the faded cloak in her hand. It had a hood, she saw, and though worn, had been often and skillfully mended. Magpie laughed upon her shoulder.

"Skittish as colts, aren't they?" she chuckled. "You'd think they'd never seen a green shoot or a bud before. What harm did they think you meant to do—bloom them to death?"

Hannah felt none of the pied bird's mirth, only a moil of sadness, puzzlement, and dudgeon. "Peace, Magpie. What am I to do?"

"I'd put that cloak on straightaway," she cackled, "if you plan on asking any other human folk where to find this Sorcerer Queen. Can't have them scattering like a pack of does every time you'd have a word."

Green Hannah fingered the patched garment in her hand. Magpie flew from her shoulder as she drew the cloak around her. It was marvelously light, the hood and neck roomy enough to conceal her flowering hair without binding. The garment had spacious sleeves, not too long, and fastened at the throat with a single loop of cord slipped over a wooden tog. Cloaked, Hannah gazed down at herself in the pool and found that with only face, forearms, and feet visible, she looked not so very different from some of the cottar women she had seen.

"What's the ruckus?" Badger demanded, waddling along the bank, followed by the fox pups. "What's all that screaming?"

Foxkith trotted not far behind them. Magpie skimmed above.

"Five girls," Hannah answered ruefully, "who fled at the sight of me. What do you think?" She smoothed the garment's subtle, muted colors, so pleasing to her eye. "If I'm to truck with human folk, it seems I must look the part."

Chapter 14
Needlewoman

Hannah walked along the upland road. Her newfound cloak concealed the green of her gown and the bloom of her hair. The way along which she walked was pleasantly leafy, the late afternoon sun balmy. Her passing raised a fine dust, further drabbing her faded cloak. Her companions fared under their own power: Magpie skirting the trees that lined the way, Foxkith and the three pups gamboling through the undergrowth beyond, even Badger ambling at roadside. Weeks of travel had worked wonders reducing the old brock's girth and increasing his stamina.

The cloak had done much to revive her spirits. People no longer gawked or fled at the sight of her. She found that, more often than not, they took her for a beggar. But she waved away all offerings, even those kindly meant, such as dippers of milk, a penny, or parings of cheese. She never touched animal fare, in any case, nor drank anything but water—and it was news she needed, not scraps or a pittance. She had only to look upon Foxkith, wildered and mute in his animal shape to recall his comely manhood and miss his human company the more keenly. No human soul she asked professed to have heard of a queenly sorceress who changed beasts into men.

As more days slipped by, Hannah found herself growing weary, downhearted once again. The travel was palatable enough, not the least bit taxing. Food was plentiful, the days fair, nights shorter and increasingly temperate. Rain fell only as brief, light showers that were never chill. Hannah found them curiously refreshing, almost as though she were drinking in the water that fell upon her skin. Yet despite her keenly pressing purpose, Hannah knew herself to be wandering, straying without direction across the fells that overlooked the moorlands running down to the sea. Sometimes she wondered who was the more lost, herself or wordless, memoryless Foxkith.

Cloaked Hannah heaved a silent sigh and paused in her pace. The stretch of road down which she and her companions traveled seemed deserted. She had not seen fellow travelers since the last village through which she had passed, just after noon. No one there had heard of Foxkith's Queen, and some had laughed behind their hands, as though finding her search absurd. The woodland girl had fared on with a heavy heart, eager to find others upon the road, perhaps more widely traveled than the staid denizens of these small upland towns.

Now, gazing back as her own road merged into another, she saw a figure making its way toward her down the adjoining road, traveling the same direction as she, but so slowly the cowled girl realized that only if she paused in her own travel would the other overtake her. As Hannah waited for the traveler to draw on, her companions melted out of sight. All of them had learned that cloak or no, Hannah elicited nearly as much human suspicion and mistrust in the company of animals as she did with green garb and flowering hair in plain view.

Magpie perched unobtrusively on a branch. Foxkith, Badger, and the fox pups peered from the brush. The traveler girl pulled her cloak more closely about her as the approaching figure drew near, a woman of middle years, straight of limb and apparently hale, but tapping a birch staff before her as she walked, almost as though feeling her way. The sun sank lower in the sky, reddening near the horizon. Drawing alongside Hannah, the woman inclined her head and murmured: "Good day to you. May the Mother save you."

"Good day," Hannah replied.

At the sound of her voice, the woman broke into a smile. "Thou'rt a lass, then," she exclaimed. "I couldn't tell. The light's grown too dim."

The cloaked girl frowned. She herself could see perfectly well in the late afternoon. "Are your eyes inflamed?" she began. "I'm a healer of sorts. . . ."

The other waved her to silence, chuckling. "Nay, none of that, my dear. 'Tis merely that my eyes are poor—poor since birth—and they grow feebler with each passing year. I'm a needlewoman. Can't see much beyond the reach of my own thread. All fuzzy beyond. Light and dark, to be sure, but no clarity. After nightfall, of course, I'm blind as a button if I'm not in good strong firelight." She laughed again, companionably and began to move on. "But come, walk with me, if thou'rt faring my way. I mustn't waste daylight."

Hannah fell into step beside the needlewoman, whose going remained painstakingly cautious, feeling with her wand.

"May I lead you?" Hannah offered. "The road's smooth."

"Why, my thanks, my dear." The other groped toward her. As the cloaked girl placed the other's hand in the crook of her arm, the woman's stride lengthened, her gait becoming firmer and more decisive. "My daughter most often leads me to and from the town," she continued good-naturedly. "But week past, the poor thing sprained an ankle, and the journey would have been too much for her. Still, I had my broideries to deliver—and I knew I'd be fine enough if I didn't dawdle or let evening overtake me. My house isn't much farther up the road past the fork. My name's Marda, by the by. And thine?"

"Hannah," the girl replied, glimpsing the fox pups and Badger skulking through the brush, keeping pace with them. Magpie flew to another branch farther up the road. Foxkith had already darted ahead.

"Pretty name!" Marda exclaimed. "I'd never heard 't. 'Tis a lovely scent thou'rt wearing." Marda's eyes, clear and gray in a face much lined by laughter, meandered over Hannah's visage. Their unfocussed journey told the girl the needlewoman could barely make her out. "Art on thy way to Linnel?"

Hannah hesitated, realized she must be referring to a town. "Is it far?"

"Nay! 'T lies not more then two hour's hike beyond my cottage. Far grander than Poder, where I left my linens to-day. I'm Linnel-bound myself on the morrow, to tabernacle. If thou'rt headed thither, thou'rt welcome to lodge with me the night. We can walk together in the morn. No need to see me home after. I've a nephew lives in Linnel who'll guide me back. Ah, here we are. What say'st?"

They had come, Hannah saw, to a withy fence washed over with white lime so that it stood out brightly even among the gathering shadows of a sun swiftly setting away. Marda waited expectantly. Hannah glanced quickly to her companions lurking among the trees. Much as she hated to leave them, especially Foxkith, even for a night, she decided she must. Never before had she been invited to share a cottar's lodging. Kind, open-hearted Marda seemed in no hurry to shoo Hannah off with a crust and a curt word—appeared, rather, ready to natter on amiably as long as her guest cared to listen. Perhaps this new-met companion could tell her something of Foxkith's enchantress. Only the evening ahead would tell.

"I thank you," the cloaked girl replied. "To lead you to Linnel in exchange for a night's lodging would be an honor."

"Merry, then!" Marda exclaimed, opening the gate and preceding Hannah up a short path to her little stone house.

On familiar ground now, the other moved with such confidence that Hannah found it easy to forget her hostess likely perceived her only as a blur. Once indoors, Marda bustled about, stirring the banked coals up into a fire for light and carving slices alternately from a great loaf of coarse brown bread and a yellow wheel of cheese while Hannah swept the hearth for her and hauled water from the well.

"There, now. Eat thy fill," Marda urged, laying the table with wooden plates and embroidered linens. Besides the bread and cheese, she served ginger beer, scraped carrots in a piquant sauce, and honeycane. Hannah relished every bite—except the cheese, which she gently declined—and hoped guiltily that her companions without were dining half so well. The ginger beer, which was very mild, nevertheless made her feel a little light-headed and strange.

"That was wonderful," the cloaked girl said as she helped her hostess clear the dishes and put them in the bucket to soak.

"Nay," Marda laughed. The pair of them moved toward the hearth to sit. "'T isn't so much the preparation as the ingredients that count. My little garden's proving most generous. The cows all brim with milk. My neighbor's got chickens that lay twice daily! 'Tis the spring come on so unexpectedly. Glorious spring."

Positioning herself in the brightest of the fire's light, Marda reached as though by long habit into a basket and drew out a little heap of plain white linens. The top one had bright stitching partway along its border. Holding it near her face, Marda took up the needle, began to continue the pattern.

"How long have you practiced your trade?" Hannah ventured.

"Yea, by the Mother," Marda laughed. "Been needling since the age of five. The world's not much use for weak eyes, but I can see quite well enough for that. Here now," she said, suddenly. "Thou'rt still swaddled in thy cloak, art not? That won't do! 'Tis much too warm to sit bundled right beside the fire. Ah." Marda leaned forward, peering very closely at the hem of Hannah's cloak. "Thou'st pulled out a bit of the stitching there." She put her own linens away. "Slip 't off. I'll mend 't."

The cloaked girl hesitated only a moment. Marda's weak eyesight would surely prevent her from seeing her guest's gown and hair clearly enough to be startled. And the other's gracious manner had already put her very much at ease. Hannah rose and pulled off the cloak. The ginger beer made her feel a little dizzy. Taking her seat once more upon the hearth, the green-clad girl handed the mantle to Marda, who shook it out and began swiftly and expertly to tack the hem.

"What a fine pea-green shade thy gown is, Hannah," the needlewoman murmured. "Small wonder thou'st worn a cloak to keep off dust. Ah, and I can just make out now whence that lovely fragrance comes. Thy hair's all woven in flowers!" Still mending, she laughed. "Well, if I'd any doubts, I've none now. Clearly thou'rt on thy way to tomorrow's fest."

"In . . . Linnel?" Hannah asked. She had resolved to tell her trusting hostess no lies.

Marda nodded. "And timed thy coming just so. They say the holyfolk will arrive tomorrow noon. Thou'st come a long way? Whence exactly—Candop? Arslay?" She gestured.

Hannah debated. "Beyond there."

"Well! Thou *hast* come far. Here. Thy cloak's done now. Just hang 't up on that peg behind thee."

Hannah did so, draping her own mended mantle beside two of Marda's own. When she turned back around—carefully, so as to keep her balance against the very slight swaying of the room—she found the other leaning nearer, peering at her.

"Now that's done, I can get a better look at thee. What beautiful tissue," she murmured, examining the many foliate layers of Hannah's emerald gown. "So fine. I can't even feel the stitches. Didst fashion this thyself? We've no cloth at all this fine hereabouts. Truly thou'rt *not* from nearby, art? How long hast been on the road?"

Hannah shifted uncomfortably beneath Marda's motherly scrutiny. "Days," she murmured.

Marda clucked and bent even closer to her guest's face. "Lady!" she exclaimed suddenly, drawing back in surprise. "Thou'rt a child—younger far than ever I guessed." And she scrambled to her feet. "Didst set out for Linnel all alone, faring days upon these wild roads without companions?"

Marda hurried to the door to check the bolt, then dropped the bar into place as well before returning to the hearth.

"Thank the Lady 'twas I thou mett'st and not some rogue," she puffed, sitting down. "Hannah, my dear, thou'rt much too young to be traveling unescorted."

The runaway girl laughed, a little too loudly, deeply touched by the other's concern. With her knack for making fire with a snap of her fingers, building thorn fences with scarcely a thought, and transforming iron into thistledown, she had never had the least qualms for her own safety. Yet loath to cause further alarm, Hannah cast about through the pleasant fuzziness settling over her brain for an explanation both truthful and plausible.

"My companions lodge elsewhere this even," she assured Marda, reaching to pat her hand. "But I longed to press on—being so close to Linnel as I found myself to be."

Marda clasped her hand briefly in return, speaking more to herself than to Hannah. "Well, thou'rt safe here. Lady's mercy!" she answered. "And the two of us traveling together should be well enough."

Reaching back into her basket, she drew out her embroidery once more, as though finding the task so familiar she could not think without it.

"But we must find thy friends in Linnel upon the morrow. Otherwise, thou must lodge with me at my nephew's." Her agitation eased. Stitching, she turned again to her guest. "But what possessed thee to fare on in such haste without thy friends?"

Hannah struggled for a fitting way to phrase her answer. She felt a little fumble-tongued. "I am in search of someone," she answered carefully. "A person unknown to me, but well known to one of my companions. He is . . . ill, and she may well be able to aid him. She is . . . some call her a sorceress, but before my friend's affliction, he spoke only good of her."

Marda nodded soberly now. "Ah, so thou'st a sick friend. What afflicts him?"

Again Hannah paused. "He's lost his power of speech," she replied at last. "His mind has wandered. He no longer seems to know my companions and me or to understand our words."

Marda bit her lip. "I see. I see. Almost as though he were enchanted—is that why thou'rt seeking this healwoman?"

Relieved, the fair-haired girl nodded, then realized Marda likely could not detect so slight a movement and added, "Yes."

The seamstress considered a few moments, sewing. "Well, I've not heard of such a one, but the holyfolk that come to the tabernacle tomorrow will be the ones to ask. They've traveled far since the advent of spring. If anyone knows of thy friend's sorceress, 'twill be they."

She stitched on, finishing the one linen, and starting another, her mood seemingly much dampened. Hannah watched her, sorry to have put the good woman in such distress. From time to time, the traveler girl had heard of holyfolk. As far as she could fathom, they were itinerant wanderers. Some, so she gathered, were plainly mad, though others seemed to be earnest souls seeking some goal which the ragged cottars living by the Tanglewood had never been able to articulate.

"Tell me of these holyfolk," Hannah urged the now-silent seamstress, seeking to draw her out. "We know little of them where I am from."

Her hostess smiled, her good humor returning. "Ah, now, my dear, they're a rare sort. Usually they travel solitary, but since the Maid's slipped free and brought back spring, they've banded, moving from town to town, 'following the footsteps of the Maiden,' so they say and telling the tale of her days."

"The . . . Spring Maid?" Hannah ventured uncertainly, thinking of the water nixie for whom the girls tending laundry among the cattails had mistaken her. Unexpectedly and to her chagrin, she found herself yawning, the fire's warmth, the ginger beer, and the cordial needlewoman's fine meal at last catching up with her. She hardly followed what Marda was speaking of now, so heavily did sleep begin to weigh on her. The old needlewoman nodded happily, perhaps in response to her guest's query, perhaps simply with her own enthusiasm.

"And of course they preach of the Lady, who embodies Maiden and Matron and Ancient Mother in one. 'Twill be quite the festival at Linnel tomorrow noon, of that thou canst be sure, for all the world's hungry for word of her. . . ."

Hannah stifled another yawn, mortified to be proving so inattentive. Marda evidently heard her and broke off.

"Ah, me, but I ramble! Forgive me. I'm alone now since my daughter married and went to Poder. She comes once weekly to walk me there, and I stay the night at her house before coming home. She'll have me living with her next, I shouldn't wonder. But enough! I'm putting thee to sleep. Thou must to bed. Come, I'll put thee in my daughter's place."

And taking Hannah by the hand, she pulled the green girl to her feet. Hannah hoped it was not apparent to Marda how much she needed the other's hand to steady her. Without it, the flower-haired girl knew she would have stumbled as her kind hostess led her to a tidy little chamber off the main room. Though small, it boasted a bed with a duck-down quilt, a dresser with pitcher and bowl, a shuttered window, and a candle in a fired clay shoe. Using a taper she had brought with her from the hearth, Marda lit the wick.

"There now. I'll be sewing in the other room for a bit. My own's beyond the kitchen. Come knocking if thou need'st."

Head nodding, Hannah stared in wonder at the bed's finely embroidered quilt and the white linen sheet Marda folded down over its edge. The woodland girl had never seen the sort of beds cottars used, only heard of them. Her own rush tick, left far behind in the little cottage beside the Tanglewood, seemed a poor thing in compare. Marda laughed as Hannah roused, running her hands over the beautiful stitching on the quilt.

"I made that for my daughter when she was just a little sprout," she said proudly. "'T tells the story of the Maiden's capture, the coming of winter. How my Gitta loved me to tell her that tale each eve at bedding."

Hannah gazed drowsily down at waves foaming about a tiny isle, at the heart of which grew a fabulous tree. A boat beached itself upon the shore. A bearded man debarked. Other panels showed the man slashing the tree with a sword, tearing off a branch and fleeing the isle. Great lacy snowflakes nearly obscured the final scene as the man's boat set sail. The odd thing was, the coverlet pictured no maid at all, only the man, his boat and blade, the island and the tree. Hannah realized with a start that she had laid her cheek against the soft stitching of the quilt, nearly asleep where she stood.

"No time for tales now," Marda chuckled. "I'll be off. Sweet slumber, Hannah. Mind thee, rise at first light, for we'll want an early start."

With a maternal pat, the needlewoman bustled off, closing the door behind her before Hannah could gather wits enough to thank her for her kindness. She heard Marda resume her seat upon the hearth, stirring up the fire again for greater light. Dazedly, the stranger girl crawled up onto the high mound of featherbeds, overlaid by the embroidered quilt, and collapsed upon it. The night was far too mild for her to need to lie beneath the covers. The fluffed mass yielded beneath her like a sigh. She sank downward swiftly and helplessly toward shapeless, half-formed dreams, captured by sleep almost before she closed her eyes.

Chapter 15
Tabernacle

She dreamed the Wizard stood before her, human-shaped but with great yellow tusks thrusting through the golden shag of his cheeks. *Come back to me, Hannah, you little fool,* he hissed at her. His lips never formed the words, and yet they sounded clearly within her mind. She tossed, frightened, unable to turn away. *Abandon your quest. It's too difficult. You'll never succeed,* he whined, almost conversational now. *Never discover the one whom you seek.* A thin strand of slaver ran from one jowl. *This besotted needlewoman cannot help you, nor her vaunted holyfolk. Whatever possessed you to think you could pass for one of them—for human?* His eyes flashed. Thunder rumbled deep in his throat. *You're not. You're a freakish thing. Like me, a sorcerous monster. I made you.* Hannah moaned, frozen with fear. Darkness surrounded them, swirling sluggishly like the dregs of a strongly steeped brew. *Return to me, and everything will be as it was before. . . .*

With a strangled cry, Hannah awoke to find morning streaming through the cracks in the shuttered window. She sat up, shaking, her head throbbing dully from last night's ginger beer. The broidered coverlet of the bed in the little room of Marda's cottage lay strewn with the petals of flowers. Their heady fragrance braced her, stilling the racing of her blood. Hannah combed one hand through her locks, remembering. The dream of the Wizard had not been her first. It had been preceded by pleasanter, if less articulate fancies: all of fallow apples swelling and young quinces burgeoning, of broad, emerald leaves brightening to saffron yellow and fields of green grass verging into gold.

It is he, not I, who is captive now, Hannah told herself firmly. The thought cheered her. She felt the darkling dream recede from her as morning light warmed her blood. Stretching, she climbed down from the bed, smoothed the coverlet, and swept the flower petals off into one hand. If he didn't fear I'd find what I seek in Linnel, he wouldn't trouble to warn me away, she reasoned. Anticipation began to fill her. After leaving the petals in a fragrant heap beside the wash basin, she splashed water onto her face, then stepped through the doorway of the little bed chamber into the other room.

"Good morrow. Good morrow," the needlewoman chattered happily, bustling about in the kitchen beyond. "Didst sleep well?"

Hannah nodded, then remembered her hostess's limited vision, and answered aloud. "Very well."

"Good, good," the other called, lifting several objects from the sideboard. Each was about the size of Hannah's hand and lapped in a gaily stitched linen. "How bright the sun shines this morn! I can almost see."

Hannah retrieved her cloak from the hearthpeg and slipped it on as Marda stowed her little bundles in a birch basket.

"Art as anxious to tread the road as I? I've tucked away our breakfast to munch as we go. Half the world will be streaming into Linnel this morn! We'd best be on our way."

Lifting the basket, she fetched her staff from beside the door, pulled the bolt, and lifted the bar. Cloaked Hannah followed her out into the morning light. Marda's flatcakes, which they ate along the road, were deliciously crisp, made of smooth starchroot flour, roughened with crushed oats and dried berries both chewy and tartly sweet. The hooded girl chatted with the needlewoman as they walked and ate, morning breeze sometimes threatening to slide Hannah's hood from her head. She held on to it, unwilling to let the wind reveal her to the world. Marda cheerily described the town ahead, detailing how they must proceed directly to the main square at Linnel's heart if they hoped to secure a place within the tabernacle itself.

"Else we'll not hear a thing the holyfolk have to say," she continued. "Thou must get us within earshot, or we'll have made our trek for naught."

Her sprightly excitement was infectious. Hannah brushed crumbs from her own smiling lips as Marda stowed the last of the empty kerchiefs back in the basket. Their pace along the broad, unpeopled road was brisk. They had not yet met another traveler. All at once, Hannah realized that she had not seen any of her own companions since the evening before. She glanced about, suddenly apprehensive, and not a little distressed to have enjoyed the merry needlewoman's company so much as to forget about the others.

"What's amiss, dear?" Marda asked, as though sensing in Hannah's silence her abrupt change of mood.

"I . . . was thinking of my companions," she murmured, truthfully enough, gazing through undergrowth and up into trees. Not a sign of Foxkith or Badger, Magpie or the fox pups did she see. "I'd hoped we might come across them on the road."

The other patted her arm. "Don't fret. They're bound for Linnel, same as we. And since they'll want to see the holy-folk on thy friend's behalf, like as not, we'll find them in or about the tabernacle. Our best course is to make good time."

"Perhaps so," Hannah murmured, troubled still. Unlike human folk, her animal companions would surely seek to avoid the press of Linnel altogether. In truth, she gauged her best hope to be catching sight of them well before she and Marda ever reached the town and resolved to keep good watch. Even brief separation—especially from wildered Foxkith—uneased her. Yet what could she do but press on and hope the others were doing the same?

Their path merged into others, and soon fellow travelers shared the road with them, many of them cloaked as was Hannah against the wind and dust. Some pilgrims were more finely dressed and better provisioned than others, having apparently come from farther away, but cottars and villagefolk—men, women, and children—all walked with an air of joyous expectancy which Hannah had never seen among those who had dwelt about the Tanglewood. Upon reflection, she realized that the farther from the Wood she fared—and the deeper into spring—the happier, more prosperous, and better fed seemed all the human folk.

The way became increasingly crowded. Some gaily beat tambors and drums as they fared along. Once or twice, fellow travelers called greetings to Marda who, evidently recognizing their voices, called cheerfully back. But the needlewoman showed no inclination to trade Hannah's company, and for that the cloaked girl was grateful. With Marda, she noticed others' eyes tended to pass over her to settle on the weak-sighted older woman on her arm. The blossom-haired girl kept her free hand about the throat of her cloak, holding the hood close about her face lest any verdure escape into others' view.

The day grew deliciously warm, the yellow light of the sun strong and invigorating as it climbed high into the sky. It had risen far to the north that daybreak, climbing along its tilted circular path. Had it not been for the gusting breeze, Hannah would have been overwarm in her cloak. The morning wore on effortlessly, buoyed by the beat of the pilgrim drums. In Marda's company, no time at all seemed to pass. Hannah found herself taken by surprise when she and all the other wayfarers streaming toward Linnel finally hove into sight of the town. The road had risen, topped a rise. All at once, Linnel lay before them, a settlement far larger than she had expected. The woodland girl guessed a thousand people must dwell in the many buildings crowding the dell before them, perhaps more. The thought took her breath away.

"What is 't?" Marda asked. The cloaked girl realized she had stopped in her tracks. Fellow travelers flowed around.

"It's bigger than I thought," Hannah managed.

Marda laughed. "We must be overlooking the town. When I was a little thing, before my eyes grew so bad, I saw 't once. 'Tis a fair-sized place! Come, we must hurry. Others are slipping ahead of us."

Again she laughed, but Hannah sensed the needle-woman was in earnest. Her trek to Linnel would be wasted if she could not get within the tabernacle, close enough to the coming holyfolk to hear their words. The younger woman started them off again, careful not to dawdle. Keeping time to the quickening beat of the drums, they made good speed down the sloping road and entered the city by late morning. Hannah felt overawed by the cobbled streets lined with plaster-and-beam houses that were two, sometimes even three storeys tall. Once out of the wind, within the shelter of the town, Hannah noticed some of their fellow travelers removing their cloaks. She held hers more tightly about the throat, fearing that by failing to remove it, she might become conspicuous—but no one paid her any heed. The noisy myriad of foot travelers all moved in a single direction, converging upon a great open space in the center of town.

A single great hall of timber and thatch, tall-roofed and high-ceilinged, occupied the square. Realizing this must be the tabernacle, Hannah guided Marda through its carven double doors. Though the hall's cool, shaded interior was not yet full, it was rapidly filling, like a dry riverbed in flood. Lightly tapping their tambors, many travelers still wore their cloaks. Hannah relaxed, no longer feeling out of place. The sound echoed off the walls. Within the great building, the press grew tighter, the milling crowd immediately separating into two halves. A central aisle remained free of all traffic, as though sacrosanct. Supporting the roof overhead, great columns chiseled from treeboles flanked the broad, open aisle which led from the entry all the way to a platform at the other end of the hall on which a simple wooden table stood, covered by a linen cloth.

"Thank the Mother," Marda breathed. "We're in. Now, child, let us thread our way forward, as close to the altar as may be."

Hannah held her tongue, acutely aware that until she had seen it standing solid and unmistakable in the middle of the square, she had had no idea what a tabernacle was. Now, though she had never heard the word "altar" before, she could only assume it meant the dais at the far end. Hannah led Marda through the still loosely dispersed crowd, which was all the while growing more populous and closely packed. The drumbeat rattled all around. She and the needlewoman were just making their way into the last quarter of the hall when a shout reached them.

"Auntie, over here!"

"Sel!" Hannah's companion exclaimed, and then to Hannah, "That's my nephew. Sweet Maiden, I'd not thought to run into him till after the fest! Lead me to him, Hannah."

The cloaked girl guided the older woman in the direction of the voice. A sandy-haired young man reached to grasp his aunt's forearm and pull her to him. Hannah made haste to follow, lest the crowd close between them.

"Auntie, I'd no notion thou'dst meant to come this day, or I'd have met thee on the road," the young man was saying, putting a sheltering arm about the older woman's shoulders. "What a crush! Where's Git?"

"Still laid by with the ankle, poor thing," Marda chuckled, patting his chest. "But as thou seest, I met this pilgrim coming from Poder yestereve, who was kind enough to lead me here."

The young man turned his frank, curious gaze on Hannah in surprise. "The Mother keep you, madam," he murmured. "My thanks for your guiding. . . ." He broke off, drawing back, startled. "Faith, thou'rt but a girl! Dost travel alone?"

"There, Sel. Don't fuss," Marda enjoined. "She lost her companions on the road day past, but we expect to come across them here at fest. She has a sick friend who . . ."

Before the good woman could finish, a cry went up outside the hall: "Holyfolk! The holyfolk—make way!"

"Already?" Marda asked above the deafening roar of words and drums.

"Yea," her nephew returned. "Word came this dawn they'd traveled late night past. 'Tis why I came so early and could find such a favorable spot. Come, Auntie. Aisle's but two paces from us, and the altar not another twelve. Shield her side, if thou wouldst, miss," he added to Hannah, still eyeing her with a certain puzzlement. "We'll keep this press off her."

Chapter 16
Holyfolk

Within the dimly teeming tabernacle, Hannah flanked the half-blind woman's right shoulder as Sel moved with her toward the nearby aisle. A group of four women before them shifted, and by sidling quickly with his aunt in tow, Sel was able to position himself, Marda, and the cloaked girl right beside a pillar lining the sunlit, open aisle. From here, they had a clear view both of the double doors at the far entry to the hall and of the low stage with the white-draped table at the hall's head ten paces in the opposite direction.

Multitudinous drumming and cheering resounded from outside, the tumult drawing nearer until it spilled into the tabernacle itself. The crowd indoors, which had grown hushed and expectant, now broke into shouts of celebration. The tambors thrummed. A man entered the hall. Dressed in a simple robe reaching nearly to the ground, he seemed not yet in middle years. The hem of his robe appeared dusty and worn from long travel, but he evidenced no fatigue, holding himself very straight as he paced forward, smiling amid the welcoming cries. Perhaps a dozen others came after him, all robed in similar fashion. Sunlight from without lit their path. The glad hubbub of the crowd followed their measured progress up the aisle.

Some were women, some men: several younger than the first; two others white-haired with age. Yet all walked with the same sense of exultation, bareheaded, chins slightly raised, gazes lifted above the ground. All carried staves. Their leader's was intricately carved. Atop its shaft, a snowflake, lily, cornsheaf, and acorn twined in a ring. Others bore single images of seedheads or pomes. Several were wrought in the shape of a girl. One looked like a little flowering tree. Holding the cloak closely about her face, Hannah gazed after the party of holyfolk as they swept serenely past, calmly at peace in the glad uproar.

"What do they look like, Sel?" Marda urged her nephew. "I can just barely make them out going by. How many?"

The young man bent to her ear to describe the dozen passersby. As the last of the procession moved beyond them, Hannah turned to the nearby platform and realized that other, more richly garbed folk now stood upon it awaiting the newcomers' arrival, apparently in welcome. Their fine raiment, vividly dyed and skillfully embroidered, set them apart from the approaching holyfolk. Hannah heard Sel murmur to his aunt.

"There on stage stand all the provost and his crew. And don't they look fine in the bright stitching thou didst put into their tunics two moons gone?"

Marda chuckled with delight. The holyfolk mounted the

platform, no more than a long step up from the floor. Their leader's hand was warmly clasped by the most elaborately dressed of those on stage, his fellows were similarly greeted, but whatever effusive words were uttered were lost amid the drumming crowd's elated cheers. When the burghers shortly filed from the stage, Hannah glimpsed them resuming their places in the forefront of the press. The leader of the holy-folk turned to address the throng, hands raised, his companions arrayed in a semicircle behind him. At once the festive multitude stilled. Even the roar from outside diminished.

"Fair solstice, good folk!" the holyman greeted them. "My companions and I have fared far to meet with you this day. I thank you for the warm welcome we have received."

His resonant voice carried throughout the hall. The crowd stood rapt. Hannah had no difficulty distinguishing his words.

"In times past," he continued, "I and each member of this band traveled alone, seeking the Divine One and her truth—often without guidance, betimes nearly in despair."

The holyman's tone quickened, the silent, attentive mass before him hanging on his words.

"Yet lately have we joined together, moving with singular purpose, our hopes newly kindled. For the signs are all around us. Who now dare doubt the Lady lives? That evil grasp which held her is broken. She is clothed now as the Summer Girl—and we, too, are set free!"

At this, the assemblage erupted into percussive cheers, wave upon wave rolling through the hall. Hannah froze, petrified, half clinging to Marda's arm—though whether to shield the older woman or be shielded by her, the hooded girl no longer knew. She stood wholly baffled by the speaker's words, deafened by thunderous noise and nearly overwhelmed by the sheer numbers huzzahing exuberantly about her. This was not a tale of which she had ever heard the cottars speak. Laughing, the holyman paused, his arms still raised, waiting patiently for the crowd's stormy approval to subside. At last, to Hannah's great relief, it did.

"All of us know," the holyman began once more, "what we learned in our cradles of the Mother and Matron who is also the Girl. It is this youngest incarnation that we seek for—so the signs tell us—it is she who walks among us now, warming the world, renewing all things, and bearing the promise of harvest in every golden step."

Nods and murmurs all around, contented jostling among the crowd. Hannah feared that in the next instant they might burst once more into shouting and rattling their drums, but the audience restrained itself, with some effort it seemed, for the holyman was speaking still.

"How she came to overthrow the wicked power that ruled her, we don't yet know. But this we mean to learn! Such is our vow: to follow in the footsteps of the Lady until we find her. Linnel is but one waystation upon our quest."

Again, a mighty roar of acclamation. Despite herself, Hannah flinched. Beside her, Marda listened, captivated. Her nephew, too, stood engrossed, though neither of them so lost to the moment as to raise their voices with the throng. The holyman spoke on, recounting how he himself received his calling to search for some person known only as the Lady, or sometimes, the Summer Girl. After him, his companions spoke, telling in turn how each came to take up the same vocation.

Their collective narrative stretched into hours, leaving the cloaked girl dazed and fatigued. She had no notion who or what this chimerical personage might be, or why these holyfolk should deem it so urgent to seek her out—or indeed, what in so doing they hoped to achieve. They were, so far as Hannah could determine, bent merely on discovering the young notable, on seeing her, convinced apparently that such would constitute fit culmination to years of toilsome searching. Hannah found it all bewildering.

The masses, however, remained heedful and vocal. Despite the high ceiling and thick thatch roof, the press crowding so closely together was beginning to make the mantled girl stiflingly warm. Those who had not been lucky enough to gain a place indoors, she knew, must feel at least as uncomfortable, standing outside unshaded on a sunny day. None of it—neither the heat nor the long hours afoot—seemed to matter a whit to the enraptured crowd.

Hannah shifted her weight, tried not to fidget. She wished she could ask Marda what the talk of the holyfolk meant, but she feared to reveal her ignorance and perhaps arouse the good woman's suspicions. As the thought recurred to her of her absent companions—Foxkith, Magpie, Badger, and the pups—whom she had not seen now for many hours, her heart swelled with impatience to be on about her own quest. At last, the oration of the holyfolk seemed to be drawing to a close.

"Help us, we pray you," their leader was saying. "Aid our search. We've heard rumors that her vernal avatar was glimpsed in Tupec not many weeks ago. Thither we hasten. Tell us whatever you've heard that may speed us, and in return we will bless you in the Lady's name. We've traveled far and are not unlearned. Ask what you will. Perhaps we may assist you in turn. Come forward, all who would ask or tell. Approach and be blessed."

The vast horde of listeners filling the hall heaved a collective sigh, and as though released by this long-awaited signal, began to move and shift. Hannah became aware that some among the crowd were making their way toward the tabernacle's door, others filtering in from outside to fill emptied space. Still others drifted forward—yet always the broad, columned aisle remained clear and unobstructed, as though to tread upon it were considered grave trespass, even in such a press.

"Now, child," Marda beside her urged suddenly. "Ask after thy friend. Haste! Go, or thou'lt miss the chance." The old seamstress patted Hannah and steered her toward the platform. "Sel and I'll await thee here. When thou'rt done, we'll set about finding thy companions."

Cloaked Hannah squeezed the needlewoman's hand in thanks and set off toward the stage. Forward passage proved nearly impossible, however. Folk near the altar, unable to exit yet, waited for those nearer the far doors to pass through before them. Hannah found herself moving against the outward flow, constantly jostled and shoved as those departing forged their way in the opposite direction. It was all the fair-haired girl could do to keep her cloak about her, prevent it from catching on passersby and being pulled askew or even torn. A well-dressed burgher moved brusquely by her. Quite unexpectedly, she found herself standing in the empty aisle.

Hannah staggered, momentarily unbalanced at the sudden absence of others packed closely about. She heard gasps from the crowd, realized in mortal chagrin that the aisle must indeed be intended solely for dignitaries. Her misstep—however inadvertent—surely constituted a transgression. Regaining her equilibrium, Hannah was hastily turning to elbow her way back into the press, when the leader of the holyfolk called out.

"Welcome! You shall be the first, my sister. Such eagerness should be rewarded. Come."

The kindness of his tone seemed to mollify those among the crowd who had taken umbrage. The cloaked girl gratefully approached the stage, where the holyman knelt to lend her his hand. He remained kneeling even after she had gained the stage, and she observed belatedly that all around her other pilgrims were, one by one, stepping up onto the platform, where each one knelt before one of the kneeling holyfolk.

Each pilgrim handed the holy one to whom he or she spoke something small, a coin, perhaps. Hannah, too, knelt down. She had no coin. Momentarily stymied, she thought of something in the next instant and slipped one hand beneath her hood—and was surprised to find herself pulling out a stalk of grain in seedhead, not the flower she had expected. Nevertheless, she pressed it into the holyman's hand. He took it graciously and murmured a word of thanks. She saw then that he was older than she had thought, no longer young, perhaps of middle years, though aging well. It was his lean, vigorous frame and inspired zeal which had, from a distance, deceived her. He eyed her curiously. Aware all at once how close she was to him, a person whose eyesight was evidently unhindered, Hannah fingered the clasp of her cloak nervously.

"Speak, sister," he urged her gently.

She scarcely knew where to begin. "Have you spent all your life in seeking this . . . the Lady?" she asked at last.

He nodded with a smile. "All my days since I received her call."

"Then I hope that you may soon accomplish your search," the hooded girl answered earnestly, then stopped, momentarily at a loss for words. Not pressing her, the holyman waited. "I, too, seek," Hannah continued awkwardly, "one who is unknown to me. She is foster-mother to a companion of mine. Some call her a sorceress . . ."

Again the kneeling girl groped, distracted, for she had become aware of something beginning to happen within her hood. Little particles, no bigger than peppercorns, were starting to sprinkle, some falling down the throat of her cloak to plink and rattle to the floor about her concealed gown. Others—fewer—slipped free of her cowl altogether and bounced along the hardwood floorboards. Grain, Hannah realized with a start: ripe seeds of barley and millet, marsh rice and rye. Still kneeling, she stiffened, drawing back, and more of the kernels danced across the floor. The holyman's gaze followed her own.

"My sister, what . . . ?" he began, but before he could finish, a commotion in the crowd below intervened.

"Stop! You pea-witted fools—"

Turning, Hannah felt her heart contract. Foxkith bounded down the tabernacle's sunlit aisle. Badger and the fox pups scrambled in his wake. Magpie swooped after, screaming at the top of her lungs. On her knees, the cloaked girl poised, frozen in horror.

"Beasts!" cried a townswoman in an outraged tone.

"Vermin from the wild," a man's voice seconded.

Another man called, "Fetch a shovel. I'll dash their brains out for defiling the holy place."

Hannah bolted to her feet. "No!" she shouted. "No, don't touch them. They're my companions!"

"Sister, calm thyself." The holyman reached reflexively to catch her sleeve as though fearing she might lose her balance and tumble from the stage. "Take care. We'll let none harm—"

As his well-meaning hand closed forcefully over her sleeve, the loose clasp at the mantle's throat gave way, and the whole, voluminous garment pulled free. Grain spilled through the air, both onto the platform and into the crowd. Hannah threw up her hands, wincing at a sudden brightness which filled the shaded hall. A moment later, she realized it was herself that glowed, or rather, her gown: no longer green, but grown yellow, incandescent as sunlight, as daffodils. Her hair, she realized in astonishment, was no longer verdant with flowers and leaves, but rife now with stalks of wild grasses and cereal corn.

The holyman kneeling beside her froze in astonishment, one hand still clutching her cloak, the other shielding his eyes. Hannah took only a moment to realize her gown was not in truth so very bright. What had seemed at first a harsh glare was nothing but a gentle glimmer. Only the suddenness of its revelation to eyes so long accustomed to a shadowy hall made it appear dazzling. Still the others upon the stage knelt stock still, as though transfixed.

In the aisle before her, Foxkith bounded to a halt, panting, stood looking up at her expectantly. Magpie circled tightly above him, cawing, her long, black tail-feathers brushing his ears. The three fox pups tumbled to a stop behind, yapping, with Badger bringing up the rear, pausing only to swipe one formidably nailed forepaw at a youth impudent enough to attempt to bundle the old brock up in his coat.

With gasps and even moans, the townsfolk sank to their knees in the glow of Hannah's gown. Cries of, "The Lady. The Maiden!" as well as, "the Summer Girl," echoed all around. Among the multitude staring in wonder or hiding their eyes, two alone still remained afoot. The half-blind needlewoman stood clutching her nephew's arm, an expression of bewilderment on her much-lined face.

"Sel, my lad," the saffron-robed girl heard Marda's urgent whisper. "What is't? What's become of Hannah? And what is that yellow light?"

Her nephew, managing to remain upright despite quaking knees, answered hoarsely, "'Tis she, Auntie. The one who lodged with thee night past. She's among us—the Summer Girl!"

All the hall heard. Hannah stood upon the platform, amazed at her own sudden transformation, weeping with the ruination of her hopes. Word of this fiasco must surely spread faster than she herself could flee. Nevermore could she hope to conceal her oddity from the notice of human folk, nevermore entreat their aid in finding Foxkith's Sorcerer Queen. Oats and seed kernels pattered from her hair. The taste of disappointment was almost too bitter to bear.

Whistling Foxkith and the others, Hannah sprang from the platform and sprinted up the aisle, pausing only to scoop brindled Badger into her arms. White-breasted Foxkith, silent and black, the laughing fox pups bright as henna streaks, and pied Magpie scolding like a kitchenwife, all followed the yellow-clad girl as she fled the hall, dashed through the great carven tabernacle doors into the brilliance of afternoon sun, and spurted away toward the cobbled town's edge through a maze of astonished revelers dispersing from the square.

Chapter 17
Golden Hannah

Golden Hannah sped across open countryside, fleeing the tabernacled town, its pilgrims and holyfolk. Tears streaked her cheeks. Her gown swirled about her vivid as candleflame. Everywhere she passed, grains of corn and barley, millet and rye rained from her hair. Gourds ripened; slender squashes swelled. Bronze pumpkins and yellow peas twined where she trod. Determined to keep well clear of human habitation, she skirted settlements, bypassed homesteads, avoided roads.

How long she ran—Badger clutched to her breast, Magpie coursing the air about her, yapping fox pups and silent Foxkith gamboling at her heels—she never knew. Time blurred, became indistinct. She took no notice of the sun's rising and setting, the cycling of the moon. Rains fell. Gentle breezes wafted. The sun-washed air grew warm as hearthside, bright as daffodils. Grasses and stalks matured to aurous seedheads in her wake, as all around her the world turned lemon and gold.

She came to a halt at last, a little weary, but more with sorrow than hard travel. The run had not taxed her, even carrying Badger. The brindled brock sat heavy in her arms, gazing calmly up at her. Nor did her other companions seem the worse for wear. The fox pups collapsed in a heap of coppery fur at her feet and promptly fell asleep, chins resting on one another's ribs and flanks. Magpie, stilled at last, fluttered down to alight, her long black tail feathers trailing elegantly from Hannah's shoulder, while Foxkith trotted in silent, mindless circles about them all, nosing the ground and chasing after voles among the corn.

Hannah found herself on a hillside thick with ripening grain. Below, a line of people slowly advanced, their scythes sweeping in short arcs, felling the crop. She saw others beyond them, harvesting, in the black alluvial soil along a little creek, blond peppers, wax beans, and mustard seed. They looked utterly different from the starving cottars she had seen about the Tanglewood—how long ago? Moons now since she had fled, green-gowned and terrified, from the Wizard's Wood. The reapers spanning the slope below her looked positively robust, their garments ample and well-mended. Smiles lit the faces of some. She heard laughter and a snatch of song. They were singing as they worked:

> "Hard hunger is over,
> Green spring sprinted past.

> Now yellowing summer's
> Bright bounty at last.
> Soon fall's russet riches
> Shall fill up our niches,
> To weather wan winter's
> Drab mantle of brown.
> All heaven is turning
> And time rearranging:
> The Maiden is changing
> Her seasonal gown. . . ."

Hannah turned. The tears upon her cheeks had dried. "Magpie," she whispered, "what does it mean? I . . . feel as though I have heard that song somehow, somewhere before—"

Laughing, the black-and-white bird gently pecked her ear. "Well, you ought to know its meaning then, oughtn't you?"

The barley-haired girl hesitated. After a moment, she seated herself, cradling Badger in her lap. Hops and sesame sprinkled from her as she shook her head. "But I don't."

The pied bird sobered.

"Neither do I, truth to tell—though I feel I *should* know it. My memory's not been sound since that boorish conjurer installed us in his Wood."

Hopping to the ground, she began snapping up Hannah's fallen seeds and throwing back her head to swallow.

"Delicious," she pronounced. "I could make a pastry with these."

In a shadowy rush, Foxkith sprang past, pronking straight into the air, then dived nose first through the grain.

Hannah heard squeaks and rustling. The snoring fox pups stirred, opened tentative eyes, then in a sudden wild scramble, bounded after him. Grain waved noisily in their wake. Clucking Magpie fluttered here and there. Hannah turned to Badger in despair.

"Lend them time enough to fill themselves," he offered, patting delicately at her collarbone. "We're all famished."

Hannah sighed, thinking of their recent, extended flight. With a rueful nod, she handed him a stalk of honeypith from her hair. He took it gratefully, began to munch.

"Gardens everywhere, now," he murmured. "Fields ready in corn. Even your hair! Such a welcome sight, to see folk tending the soil."

Hannah stroked his silvery head. "How long . . ." she started, changed her mind. "How far do you think we've come?"

Badger shrugged. "Who knows? A very great way, I'd wager. More than you guess."

The yellow-robed girl twisted nervously at a ripe oat stem nodding among her hair. "No more than an hour, surely? No farther than a handful of miles. . . ." She let the words trail away as Badger shook himself. She stammered, "I meant only to ensure the townsfolk didn't pursue us."

The old brock nuzzled her arm. "Dear girl, I think you put them behind you in the first three strides. Shall I tell you how our last passage seemed to me? To me, it seemed we hurtled along, leagues at a step, for flickering days and nights, wrapped in a filmy aureole of rainbow hue. Had I been in any other's hands but yours, sweet bud, it would have frightened me."

Hannah stared at the ancient creature, debating whether, like Foxkith, he had abandoned his senses.

"No," she whispered. "Surely you dozed and dreamed."

But the brindled brock only shook his head, lapping industriously at the sweet sticky sap of the honeypith on his whiskered lips. "Look at the sun," he said. "See how it tilts across the sky to stand near directly overhead at noon? Was that the way it shone the day we came into Linnel, when it rose due east, veering away to the south as it climbed?"

Hannah shook her head, apprehending for the first time how far north the sun's path had moved since—when? An hour gone? Yesterday? No, surely today could not be the same day as that on which she had fled Linnel. She grasped it now. But how had this come about? Astonishment rendered her speechless, lost. Badger nuzzled her.

"Dear one, ever since you began to defy your Wizard, I've deemed you to be much more than you seem, more yet than you know, far more than any poor beast such as I could ever guess."

Hannah sat in silence, gazing down at the radiant tissue of her citrine gown, at the gay seed-headed grasses intermingling ever more profusely with her straw-colored hair. The reapers' song spoke of spring, summer, and winter. Were they all—what was the word Magpie had used among the bulrushes—seasons? Magpie left off feeding and bounced up pertly beside Badger, began combing through his fur as though searching for fleas. He huffed at her indignantly. Laughing, she retreated to perch on Hannah's knee. The yellow-garbed girl stroked her absently, lost in thought.

Foxkith trotted by, bringing the fox pups voles. Sleepy

once more, they bolted them down. What had the cottars called her that day she had visited their village: the Winter Damsel? She had had no notion what they had meant by it at the time. And the girls with the laundry baskets had spoken of a Spring Maid and, perhaps, mistaken her for that wight—as lately the folk of Linnel had believed her the Summer Girl. Surely they had deceived themselves. Hadn't they? She had heard with her own ears the preposterous tale the holyfolk had told. It had nothing to do with her. Nothing at all—did it? Below, the reapers continued to gather and sing. Hannah shivered.

"What becomes of me?" she wondered aloud. "Magpie, what am I now?"

"Well, I don't know," the bird answered conversationally. "What are you? What are we all?"

"I meant," the wheaten-haired girl answered stiffly, giving the other a sour look, "why am I no longer as once I was?"

"True enough, and a good thing, too," Magpie chirped. "Nor am I as once *I* was, for that matter. Nor Badger. Nor the foxlings—nor our fine gallant Foxkith. We're all of us changing."

"But it's I who am changed the most!" Hannah insisted.

The pied bird cocked her head. "Pity we can't ask if Foxkith agrees. At least we still recognize you. Had I not seen with my own eyes, I'd never dream our swart foxy companion could once have been your errant young man. Now there's a change! It's no good carping. You needn't feel so put upon."

Hannah carefully set Badger on the ground and hugged

her knees. Grain fell as she nodded to the folk reaping below. "I'm not at all like them anymore."

Magpie shrugged. "You were never much like them."

"Not so," Badger protested, delicately pawing at Hannah's arm. "Much of you's very like the cottars still."

"But now they fear me," the yellow-robed girl began.

"They always feared you," the pied bird exclaimed.
"They're a pack of idiots—"

With a snort, the Old Badger leaned to cuff her lightly
from Hannah's knee. Magpie bounded to earth with a
squawk and hopped about chirring. Hannah sighed.

"I thought they feared the Wizard, or the Wood. Then
the Golden Boar. But I never thought to find them so afraid
of me."

She felt dangerously close to tears again.

Badger patted her hand. "I don't think it fear so much as
awe, child. Your cures and charms, your hair, your fearless-
ness of the Wood: all reasons they were in awe of you."

"Not I," Magpie snapped.

"Nor we!" one of the fox pups yapped gaily, licking his
lips. Foxkith turned to look at her, his posture expectant, his
dark, roving eyes bright. But never a sound did he utter.

"In awe of you and your gifts," Badger concluded.

"Gifts," Hannah murmured. The word sounded so odd.

"Let's tally," Magpie countered, fluttering up onto her
shoulder, out of Badger's reach. "You can heal. You're never
short of food, even in times of great want. You were once a
wizard's ward. You've an odd gown, and green things grow
in your hair."

The grassy-haired girl nodded tentatively, picked up her thread. "I know a little magic—can kindle fire, and whistle a broom, change pebbles into radishes."

"And build a thorn fence in a trice," Magpie agreed. "Growing things spring up wherever you tread."

How could she do those things? Hannah wondered. No one had taught her. All that was needed, it seemed, was for her to clear her mind and quiet her heart, and the knowledge simply came to her.

"Sweet child," Badger added, "I think you've scarcely delved the surface of your powers."

"You run like the wind, leagues at a step, and sweep others along in your wake," the bird on the golden girl's shoulder rattled on. "Compress days into minutes—"

"And I can see!" Hannah exclaimed. "How far—I never realized before. . . ."

Rising, she stared into the distance and saw many miles beyond the range of what her vision, enclosed within the Tanglewood, had ever been. The farther she gazed, the more her sight expanded, like that of an eagle rising into the air, to encompass vast spans, even those beyond horizon's rim. All she saw was sharply delineated, details minutely defined: reapers laughing and chatting, wiping the sweat from their brows; boys herding goats; girls crabbing in a marsh; men weeding and milking; women churning or weaving or suckling their babes.

She saw geese gleaning yellow weeds, deer browsing a copse of saplings with trembling, brassy-bright leaves, grasshoppers fleeing the ponderous hooves of dun cattle.

Buff-winged herons snapped up tawny frogs. A spotted ounce stalked golden hares deep in a mountain glade. But everywhere she saw ripening fields, some already mature enough for harvest, ready as the one in which she now stood, rapt, rooted like a tree.

Far distant, inestimably far, at the very limit of her vision, she beheld the Tanglewood—but not the leafless, lightless Wood of old. Once-dormant trees now stretched fully in leaf, their twisted branches gentled by foliage. Haygrass lined the glades, streams, and thickets of bright, plump berries. Blonde Grizzled Bear rummaged one such, her belly burgeoning. Rain Crow skulked the riverbank, grumbling at the dearth of carrion. A profusion of songbirds rushed among the boughs. Tiny flying squirrels glided from trunk to trunk. Crayfish scuttled the pools. Crickets trilled and jingled from the reeds.

Only at the Tanglewood's heart did darkness yet lie: a twisting labyrinth of thorns, dense and overgrown. Within its tunnels roved the Boar, golden gleaming as the heaps of treasure all around him, trapped by thorns. Though restless with rage, shouldering coffers of coin and jewels, he seemed worn, unsteady on his feet, his once great strength now too far dwindled to allow him to force his way past the intertwining spines of his barbed prison. Now and again he let loose a pealing roar that rattled the ground, rumbling like thunder which, Hannah fancied even here, so far removed, she could still faintly hear.

She turned her gaze up, into the sun-bright sky, found her vision seeking, searching, stretching beyond the blue vapor of atmosphere to a dark vastness beyond, where comets traversed unimaginable spaces and planets traveled in sweeping arcs. The cast of the stars had changed, just as the slant of the sun's path had. How odd for such a slow thing, a process so gradual, to have taken place in the brief hour of her flight from Linnel. She was not at all sure what this retilting of the sky might mean. She had not caused it: she knew so much. But something within her must, she felt sure, have caused both her and her companions to experience the passage of many days as only a fleeting moment. Slowly, as one caught in a dream, she turned her gaze back to earth, to the old brock at her feet.

"Badger," she whispered, suddenly frightened, "am I human?"

"Not quite inhuman, if that's what you mean," Magpie harumphed, interrupting. Hannah eyed her doubtfully. The pied bird chuckled. "Well, I'm not human either, if it cheers you."

"I think it must be that what you are goes far beyond the commonplace," Badger offered.

"But what possesses me?" Hannah exclaimed. The abundant seedheads among her fair locks riffled and bowed. Her sun-colored garment fluttered gently in the same breeze. Very softly, Magpie seized in her beak Hannah's ear as though by doing so she could make the other understand.

"Nothing 'possesses' you," the bird tartly insisted. "You are simply becoming whatever you were always meant to be and don't yet know yourself."

Hannah fingered her ear, brushing Magpie's black beak lightly aside, turning so she could see the bird. "Do you think Foxkith's Sorcerer Queen can explain my own transformation?"

"There's a thought!" her winged taunter exclaimed. "But are you certain you'll want him put back once more into human shape, having just convinced yourself of your own 'inhuman' nature?"

The sulfur-clad girl stared at the pied bird. "Of course I do!" she cried aghast. "I want Foxkith himself again."

"Then, dear child, shouldn't you want exactly the same good for yourself," Badger interjected quietly, "to be what it is you are, what you were always meant to be?"

Hannah paused, sobered. A new determination began to form in her. "But how am I to find his Queen?" she murmured. "Foxkith can't say. The animals don't know. Human folk have never heard of her—"

"Ask yourself, then," said Magpie curtly. "Find your own path. Follow your heart. Where does it lead you?"

Hannah stood, considering. Now that she had stopped her ceaseless travel, coming to rest for the first time in she knew not how long, she could indeed feel a subtle tugging within her breast, an infinitesimal pull upon her pulse's tide. It turned her south. The slope of the hillside lay below, with its reapers; and beyond that, the creek at the bottom of the vale; then the edge of the uplands, the moorlands and heaths; and finally the sea, where towers of white cloud stood, marking some spot faraway beyond horizon's edge. An island, perhaps. Perhaps a distant shore.

Straightening to wipe her brow, one among the reapers spotted her. The woman cried out, suddenly catching sight of canary-bright Hannah, standing like a beacon in the heat-shimmered air.

"The Girl!" Her cry came faint from down the hill. "Look you, the Summer Girl!"

Others among the reapers looked, some pointing, some hallooing. Several dropped their tools and began to ascend the slope, gesturing and exclaiming. The fair-haired runaway watched, oddly calm, without the slightest qualm of panic now. The snoozing fox pups woke, leapt to stand barking down at the advancing folk. Foxkith braced, tensely alert. Badger settled himself contentedly at Hannah's feet as Magpie dug her hard little toes into the girl's quince-colored shoulder.

"Well?" she said impatiently. "Do you know yet where we're to go?"

The reapers neared. "Lady! Maiden!" they cried.

Hannah laughed. "Yes," she answered. "I do."

She whistled once to Foxkith and the pups. The dark fox sprang to her heels, the foxlets half a bound behind. Magpie took wing. Smiling, Hannah scooped Badger into her arms and stepped forward, downhill, toward the approaching folk. All in an instant, it seemed, she grew vast: infinitely grander in scale—yet at the same time far more tenuous, less palpable, much more difficult to perceive. Her stride, which felt no more than a normal step, carried her over the reapers, beyond them, far down the hill. She felt the diaphanous substance of her gown pass through them like sunlight, like a warm, sweet breath.

Her next stride took her across the valley toward the uplands' edge. Foxkith and the others traveled with her, borne along like mayflies in a breeze. She stepped down from the uplands as easily as alighting from hearthstone to the kitchen floor. Wild moorlands and heath thick with blooming gorse slipped by in a trice, a heartbeat, no time at all. Everywhere her diffuse, radiant foot trod—never so much as bruising a blade of grass beneath the weightless wind of her passage—the lush profusion of vegetation now blanketing the land turned mellow, pale saffron to topaz to burnished gold, seasoned and ripe. Grain cascaded from her hair like glittering, gilt rain. Barely a dozen pulsebeats passed till Golden Hannah found herself and her companions upon the smooth gray shore of the sunlit sea.

Chapter 18
Faraway Shore

Hannah stood upon the broad, flat beach, her own familiar size and heft once more, no longer looming and sweeping and ethereal as a wind. Foxkith poised before her, nose up, ears pricked, as sharply taut as if he had just dropped from the sky. Magpie lit upon the knobby crest of a great, empty whelk. Gaily oblivious, the yapping red foxlets tumbled over the gray sand beneath her feet. Badger heaved a sigh of relief as she knelt to set him down.

All around them lay the wide, smooth strand. Shore grass heavy in seedheads nodded. Beyond, the jewel-bright sea foamed in, throwing spray. Sun glittered on pounding, cerulean waves. No thunder now but the booming tide. The tower of cloud loomed at horizon's edge, rising lofty and sheer as the trunk of some pale-barked tree. The column flared, fanning at the top like a spray of branches enveloped in snowy blooms.

Foxkith stood transfixed, staring at it. Then in a sudden burst, he came to life, erupting into the air like a stormbolt, but silent and dark as coal. Lightning swift, he streaked up the beach toward the distant clouds still waxing and burgeoning like a stately, numinous tree. Hannah stared after the dwindling blur that a moment before had been her swart fox ready to hand. An instant later, yipping and hooting, the ruddy fox pups galloped after him. Magpie flushed, calling. "He's off. Best follow!"

Hannah stooped to gather Badger, but he waved her off.

"Don't trouble. I've had quite enough for now of being ported about. Run on. I'll catch you up. See? He's not bolted so very far."

Straightening, yellow-robed Hannah saw that Foxkith had indeed come to a halt. She could not make out what arrested his attention: some object embedded in the sand. A hundred paces up the beach, he and the fox pups circled busily. Magpie fluttered above. The grassy-haired girl trotted toward them, her gait normal. No need for prodigious strides now. She heard Badger whiffling along, falling farther and farther behind. As she drew near, Golden Hannah gazed intently at the spot Foxkith and the others orbited. The voiceless dogfox began to dig vigorously. Hannah knelt, peering, but still could not make it out.

"What's this?" she asked, though she expected no reply.

Since the Wizard had forced him into this vulpine shape, the young knight's thoughts had wandered far. He rarely acknowledged her speech, often seemed not to have heard the words she uttered. Yet this time, he met her eyes, almost as though he understood. Hannah stroked the soft down of his ebon fur. He nipped her hand ever so lightly and returned to digging. One of the fox pups scratched tentatively. Hannah caught up an oyster shell and began to shovel away sand, as Magpie called instructions from the smooth carapace of a horseshoe crab half a dozen paces off.

"What have you found?" Hannah asked Foxkith again.

Again he looked at her, licked her hand, and returned to pawing at the sand. The foxlets chased tiny turtles into the sea. Foxkith paused, glanced out across the spuming surf toward the distant, lofting cloud. Hannah managed to slip her fingers under the edge of whatever they excavated and pry it up. The dark fox at once returned his attention to her, sniffed urgently at the artifact. It was wood, she saw, scoured gray by sand and brine: no mere floating limb, but squared and shaped—broken at one end.

"This is part of a boat," she exclaimed.

Wheezing, Badger waddled to inspect the silvery thing and sneezed. "Phew! It smells of sorcery."

Foxkith bounded away. The other two pups had abandoned their turtles for something else embedded in the sand. The black fox pounced, grasped the item in his teeth, pulling at it and digging. Leaving the first piece with Badger, Hannah went to Foxkith and helped him free the second: an oarlock. They had found the hull of a wreck, she realized, beached by the tide. Piece by piece, they unearthed its split keel, part of the broken gunwale, numerous splinters and pegs, a snapped oarblade, the anchor stone, and the black figurehead that had crowned the prow: large as a gourd, weighty as brick—a carven fox's head.

For another half an hour, Foxkith ran about the beach,

nose to the sand, but evidently could discover nothing more. At length, he returned to Hannah. She noticed only then that he had indeed found something else, which he carried in his mouth: a small, flat object smaller than the compass of her palm, in which he laid it. But unlike the other items they had recovered, this article was metal. The shadow fox sat on his haunches, gazing up at the flaxen-haired girl as she examined the thing.

Argent, much pitted by surf and sand, its shape was nonetheless familiar: a rim encircling a tree simultaneously in flower, leaf, and fruit. With a little thrill of recognition, Hannah laid it beside their wooden finds. It was a cloakpin, exactly like the mate her lost knight had worn that first hour she had laid eyes on him, upon a beach very much like this one, so long ago—a dark young man on a fair white steed ramping the strand below the Tanglewood.

"This was your boat, Foxkith," she murmured, fingering the bits and pieces before her, "wasn't it? You came by sea from your Sorceress's hold—and landed here."

The jet-black fox sprang forward, seized Hannah's jonquil-colored gown in his teeth and tugged, as though to pull her toward the waves. Still kneeling, she let him. After a moment, he let go, stood gazing fixedly over one shoulder at the far-off cloud. There, beyond the reach of even Hannah's vision, on the very edge of the sunlit world, perhaps an island drifted. Wind surged against her cheek. Gulls cried high overhead. Limitless ocean seethed below. She could not be sure.

"Where lies your Queen?" she asked. "On some isle across the running sea?" He trotted to the waves' edge, turned, trotted back to her. "Foxkith, do you understand my speech? Have you begun to remember yourself?" She reached toward him, but he shied from her touch, still skittish as a deer. Hannah rose, hands on her hips. "But how am I to reach such a place?" she exclaimed. "I doubt even my newfound powers lend me knack enough to tread seafoam."

She had laid the cloakpin down, traded it for one of the wooden splinters. Frustrated and perplexed, she gazed at the fragment in hand, then felt her fingers tighten about the silvery piece of drift. She blinked, frowning, as the figure of a woman slowly formed in the grain, almost too subtle to discern. The hem of the apparition's gown trailed down and down. Raised arms and streaming hair fanned upward out of sight. At Hannah's feet, Foxkith waited restively. She stroked the wood. The clarity of its faint, feminine outline waxed, waned, focused, and diffused. The odor of sorcery, pungent as basil, pervaded her senses.

"Your Sorcerer Queen conjured this," she whispered, "this entire ship to ferry you to shore. Here you beached and stowed—but since then, storm and tide have torn your craft to bits." Foxkith circled her twice, then sat again. The fair-haired girl murmured, "What use am I to make of it now?"

Mute, the dark fox made no sound, nor moved, merely gazed at her. Thwarted, she let her hand drop, the wooden fragment falling to the sand. Foxkith snatched it up, stood on tiptoe, paws against her gown, pressing the shard back into her palm. Hannah took it numbly. He sat back down again, snorted, cocked his head. Hollow, hopeless, Hannah watched him, unable to fathom what he wanted of her. Time passed. Gradually, growing still within herself, she became aware of the soft, regular pulsing of her own heartsblood.

And all at once she knew. From deep within, the method came to her. Without another thought, the yellow-garbed girl brought the piece of driftwood to her lips and breathed upon it. Foxkith sprang up again, standing on toes. As Hannah watched, the dove-gray hue of the driftwood deepened, the shard growing heavy in her hand. Miniature gunwales sprouted along a curved hull with a raked stern and upswept bow. The tiny craft took shape within her grasp, no bigger than the toys with which cottar children played. The figure topping the bowpost was a minute fox's head, exactly like the one they had found earlier in the sand, only infinitely smaller.

Fascinated, Hannah gazed down into the hold, then staggered suddenly as the minuscule boat swelled, tilting in her arms. Foxkith sprang away from her. Alarmed, she dropped the expanding craft. It thudded to the sand, spreading and enlarging until the beam had grown as broad as Hannah was tall. The length of keel stretched nearly twice that measure, deeply bedded in the sand. A sapling straight as a boar spear soared from the open bow. Magpie flew to perch on it. Badger chewed one paw meditatively. Foxkith and the copper pups milled.

White sea dashed in about them suddenly, dissolving the strand. Laughing, Hannah saw the now life-sized craft tip, sway. Snatching up a startled Badger, the citron-clad girl dropped him into the hold. Whistling the fox pups, she pitched them in as well. Foxkith sprang, scaling the lapstraked curve of the hull, and scrambled to the prow. Magpie fluttered cawing as Hannah herself clambered aboard.

Moments later, backrushing waves dragged the keel free of shore. The craft spun lazily in the surging tide. Above, a long sail, fine and pale as gauze, unfurled from the mast tree. The emblem it bore was a flowering hardwood, heavy in fruit and leaf, the trunk of which had a woman's form. Air filled the sail. The pied bird found a perch atop the vulpine figurehead, which seemed to lean into the wind as the sorcerous craft pivoted, heading out to sea.

The sunbright swells ran rough and wild. The silvery vessel slipped graceful as a ghost between roiling waves. Golden Hannah seated herself, Badger dozing in her lap, the fox pups huddled about her feet, Foxkith watchful in the prow, long-tailed Magpie hunkered above. The yare little craft steered swift and unerringly toward the rising cloud. Afternoon waned, until at last, Hannah was able to make out an island beneath the cloud. The jet-dark fox tensed at the sight of pale, distant cliffs barely perceptible through boiling surf.

Westering sun declined, falling due west into the sea and turning Hannah's yellow gown to amber as they neared the lofty escarpments of the isle. She knelt in the prow beside Foxkith now, feeling oddly wistful, weary with hard travel. Badger lay curled up and snoring among the fox pups. As dusk fell, the billows calmed. The cloud tree looming above the isle glowed vivid salmon. A hint of coolness nipped the air. As the apricot sun doused itself and the sea all around them burned, the craft turned nimbly in toward shore. Slowing to a drift, it eased through the shallows, ploughing smoothly aground without even jarring.

The fair-haired girl roused herself, shook Badger awake. A splash told her Foxkith had already sprung down from the gunwale. Peering over the side, Hannah saw skates and fingerlings glide through the bronze-colored, ankle-deep tide. One by one, she handed the fox pups over, then carrying Badger, waded ashore herself. Foxkith shook out each wet, midnight paw in turn while Magpie stalked fiddler crabs. The ruddy foxlets, sleepy still, sat nibbling their shoulder fur. The old brock, when Hannah set him down, stretched yawning as the silverwood dinghy, herbaceously aromatic, dispersed silently into flotsam in the lapping waves behind.

As the last rays of dying sunlight faded, Hannah spotted the ruins of many boats upon the broad, curving strand. They had the look not of shipwrecks, but of a fishing fleet, beached for the night years upon years ago by folk who had vanished never to return. Other remains scattered the beachhead, very much fallen into disrepair: tall posts that could have served for the stretching or drying or mending of nets, what might once have been tables for the gutting and cleaning of fish. Little storage sheds leaned here and there, most nearly collapsed, their contents—caulking tools and pots of tar, cork floats, trays of fishhooks, spare shuttles of line—undisturbed save by wind and weather.

Darkness fell before she could observe more. Bushels of stars now blazed overhead. The evening air was cool. Drying in the salt breeze, Hannah's gown felt papery, a little stiff. She eyed the sheer cliffs, pearly and luminescent even in darkness, rising before her and her companions. What had become of the folk who once had frequented this shore? she wondered. Where had they gone? The whole scene had filled her with a strange nostalgia, a longing she could not name. Foxkith was already trotting across the sand, past the battered ships and wooden wreckage, toward the cliffs.

"I suppose we must follow," Hannah murmured, oddly reluctant to stir.

Foxkith picked his way along a narrow track which threaded steeply up. Hannah climbed behind, pursued by waddling Badger and the fox pups, with Magpie hopping and hying the others along. The starry sky turned slowly on its hub. Gazing deep into clustered patterns, Hannah picked out the shapes of Rain Crow and Blonde Grizzled Bear, cottars and holyfolk. No moon shone. Only the stars and the fireflies gleaming in her wheaten hair illuminated their path. Night deepened. Hannah lost track of time. Her limbs felt heavy, she knew not why. Morning, gray as thistledown, stole gradually across the sky. Hannah glimpsed Foxkith disappearing beyond the cliff's crest up ahead. A moment later, she realized they had reached the top.

Chapter 19
City

Hannah stood at the top of the cliffs as the cool, amber light of dawn washed over her. Before her stretched a rocky expanse, a wide plateau made of the same chalky stone as the cliffs. The whole place was very nearly barren, scarcely a weed or a spindle of grass to be seen. Badger stirred heavily in Hannah's arms. Before her, the russet foxlets sniffed chinks and crevices in the stone. Magpie alighted in the dust a few paces ahead of Foxkith, who stood testing the wind, his eyes closed to the sighing breeze. The high air here was chillier than that of the strand. Hannah shivered.

Foxkith found his bearings. Swift as a raven, off he sped, cutting obliquely inland across the gentle curve of cliffs following the arc of shore below. The red foxlets flashed after. Magpie took wing. Badger, with a disgruntled sigh, merely tucked his nose beneath his paws as Hannah shifted him and set off in pursuit, her pace no more than an easy walk. Fatigue nipped at her, and prudence, too. Again, the wind smelled of sorcery. She ambled along, in no great hurry, confident that she could not long lose Foxkith within the confines of the isle. She wanted time to look over the odd place to which they had come.

It was rocky, open, neither markedly hilly nor particularly flat. The terrain was rough though, requiring stamina to cross. No signs of human habitation met her eye, no roads or homesteads, no evidence of recent fire, no castoff scraps or broken implements lying discarded along her route. The emptiness of the place troubled her. She and her companions found themselves traversing a vast wasteland unlike any they had encountered since fleeing the Tanglewood. More worrying still, her hair was no longer thronged with greening shoots which, falling to the ground, could take root and spring up into grass and groundcover, saplings and vines.

Instead, her wheaten locks felt strangely lifeless. The barley and millet, wild rice and corn there drooped, tattered, beating in the constant wind, the seedheads no longer fat and full but ragged now, losing their grain. The vivid yellow of her gown seemed to be fading, bleeding away to reveal a darker, more henna-like hue. The garment rustled as she walked. Hannah hugged Badger and tried not to think about it, unwilling to draw any hasty conclusion. She was here now, and there was nothing that could be done about it. The whole island smelled of sorcery, faint and faded, very ancient, perhaps, but sorcery no less. She felt fatigue increasing as the journey wore on.

Few beasts appeared, and those all shabby, thin: dormice peering from the rocks, a chevron-patterned snake, a handful of sparrows scratching the dust.

"Ho," Hannah called after them. "Good morrow! I'm a stranger to this place—come in search of one who, among her folk, is both sorcerer and queen."

None returned her greeting or even paused, though some gazed at her in a way that told her clearly that they understood her, could have answered had they willed. They seemed to glance past her, as one might do a fallen limb or an empty husk, to disregard her words as one would the soughing of wind or the babbling of a stream. Hannah drew back, slightly alarmed. The air of preoccupation about these creatures was fiercely palpable. They reminded her of nothing so strongly as the enchanted knights who, one after another until Foxkith had arrived at her blooming, had passed her by without a second glance.

All appeared to be searching for food with a single-mindedness that was almost febrile. Those Hannah approached flitted away. The stranger girl stared after them, dumbfounded. How many months had it been since she had seen fellow creatures in such a case? They were close to starvation, surely. Yet when she reached to her hair to find some sustenance to offer them, she found nothing, her seeds gone, blown away.

She shivered harder in the cool, thin breeze, determined not to panic, not to mention her odd affliction to her companions unless she must. After all, what could they do? Before the Wizard had enchanted him, Foxkith had never spoken any ill of his Sorcerer Queen, insisting that she had been a kind, loving, noble mistress—despite the number of his fellows she had sent to their doom. Hannah cast about her uneasily, feeling not so much watched as the inexplicable sense that this cheerless place, the whole vast and sorcerous isle, was drinking her in, slowly, dram by dram, the deeper into its heart she tread. Guardedly, she walked on.

Unexpectedly, she stumbled across a road, human-laid of stone, but long untrod. Badger in her arms dozed on. Long-tailed Magpie winged ahead of her. Faint barking sounded from the fox pups far to the fore. She had lost all sight of Foxkith, but harbored no doubt he must be making for the city that now loomed dimly in the distance. Hannah's heart quickened. Surely here she would find her foxed friend's Sorcerer Queen, some explanation for her own distress. Despite her growing malaise, she spurred her pace— only to discover, as morning sun climbed, casting better light, that the city stood deserted before her.

As she entered the vast settlement, the wayfarer girl stared at the ruined buildings, all made of the same pure white stone as the cliffs. Many plinths and columns, arches and interlocking blocks lay tumbled now, as though some mighty shaking of the earth had rattled them apart. Timber roofs slumped, some fallen to decaying heaps. Fire had blackened certain door-beams, scorched walls—yet that did not seem the cause of the site's destruction. Rather, it appeared to Hannah that some cataclysm had driven the inhabitants off within a very brief space of time and that here and there cookfires, untended and undoused, had subsequently burned out of hand.

Furnishings within the dwellings remained undisturbed, if faded and rotting. That animals had long since occupied rooms with roofs still intact was evident from tracks and nests, occasional bones—but none were human bones.

Here the odor of sorcery, though ancient, was very strong. Hannah wandered through the great dilapidated city, searching, calling. No answers came, either from human or animal voice. She gazed about her at fallen stones, unsure now whether the crumbling collapse had come about in an instant, or gradually over time. But what had become of the inhabitants? she wondered anew.

"Surely they did not leave by sea," she found herself musing, as she sank down to regather her strength upon an overturned capstone in a large square. "Their boats remain on the shore below."

Badger woke, sat up, began combing his brindled fur. Magpie appeared, alighted on the other end of the coping. Hannah gazed at the buildings across the square, one of which—the largest—sported carvings upon its side: scenes of fisherfolk, festive drumming processions, artisans, and tillers of the soil. She had seen so many carvings now, on houses and shops, stables, a forge, often on buildings much larger than the rest, especially here at the center of town, grand structures the functions of which she could not discern.

Opposite the great carved palace rose a hall similar to the tabernacle in Linnel, though this was larger and made of stone. One wall had collapsed, most of the roof long since fallen away. What little ceiling remained glinted with golden stars. Stone columns left standing within were carved in the shape of trees. Hannah turned to her companions. Magpie sat with feathers fluffed, although the air was merely cool, not cold.

The pilgrim girl inquired wearily, "What do you make of this place?"

The pied bird gave a little start. "It uneases me," she muttered. Thunder rumbled in the distance, from the far mainland that had once been Hannah's home.

"Because of the destruction here?" she asked. "Because human inhabitants are nowhere to be found?"

The other shivered. "No. It's all familiar somehow. It stirs my memory in an eerie sort of way."

"Mine, too," Badger groused. "As though I've but lately awakened from dreaming, only to find myself dreaming of it still."

Hannah set him on the cobbled ground to stretch his limbs. Besides her growing sense of alarm and increasing fatigue, she had begun to feel another disquiet—not foreboding exactly, a more elusive sensation: banished remembrance or a just-forgotten reverie. She cocked her head.

"How do you mean? Have we heard of this place before?"

Magpie preened one wing in agitated silence.

Badger shook himself. "No. Not that. I think—" He raked his fur distractedly. "I can't think how."

"Nor I," the black-and-white bird added. "But I'll ponder as we search. Odds! Where's that Foxkith taken himself? And where, besides, is his Sorcerer Queen? The whole isle seems vacant and void as an old eggshell, for all it reeks of sorcery."

Surprised at her vehemence, Hannah reached to smooth Magpie's ruffled feathers, but she hopped away. The questing girl sighed. When first they had arrived—had it been less than a day ago?—she had hoped that, topping the cliffs, they might encounter those able to direct them to the Sorcerer

Queen. Yet all they had found was barrenness, desertion, and ruin—though Foxkith had seemed quite at home. At the very least, she had expected to follow the swart fox's lead. Now he was nowhere to be seen. The three red foxlets trotted into the square from behind a mound of rubble. They looked thirsty and spent.

"Where's Foxkith?" Hannah called.

"Gone!" one of them threw back. "Gone on!" his companion chorused, while the third sang, "Outrun!"

"Couldn't any of you keep pace?" Magpie queried irritably. "How are we to find him now in the midst of all this rubbish?"

"Peace," Hannah breathed, stroking the fox pups as they slouched up panting and threw themselves loose-limbed at her feet. She had no strength to spare for bickering. "Let's all rest a bit and think what to do."

Badger scratched his ear. "Are you in doubt, child?" the old brock asked shyly. "Maybe your heart mistook the path?"

Magpie laughed harshly. "Fie! Foxkith sought to come here, too."

The old brock shrugged. "Perhaps our ghostly vessel beached the wrong strand?"

The black-and-white bird chirred raucously. "Hannah, Foxkith, and the boat—all three couldn't be wrong."

The straw-haired girl shook her head. "Foxkith rejoiced at our landfall. Surely this is the destination he sought—though how much altered since last he set foot here?"

Dispirited, she cast about. No way to tell. She had no idea now which direction Foxkith had gone. Sitting gave her no strength, only chilled her further. Rousing herself, she told the others, "Still, he ran off in search of *something*. We, too, must find it. With luck, it will be his Sorcerer Queen."

"I suggest we part," Badger offered. "I keep feeling odd twinges of memory, but I know I'll never succeed in recalling amidst all these clucks and chattering."

Magpie cawed rudely at him till Hannah took her gently in hand.

"I agree. The city's immense. Thousands once dwelt here, surely. We'll cover more ground searching separately." Trying to sound neither discouraged nor discouraging, she added, "Much lies beyond the city as well—for all we know, Foxkith dashed straight through. Let's scatter and meet back here at dusk."

Old Badger nodded. The fox pups snorted and licked their chops. Magpie pecked at Hannah's hand till the fair-haired girl tossed her carefully into the air, giving her first choice. Straight as a dart, the black-and-white bird sped west. Badger nodded to the south.

"I'll backtrack a bit." He waddled off.

Hannah stroked the fox pups' heads.

"Will you rove north when you've caught your breath?" They grinned and nosed her hand. She herself turned eastward, into the wind. "I'll head this way and see you all upon this spot at day's end."

※

Hannah roved eastward, calling at intervals, to no reply. She found herself relieved, almost guiltily so, to be shed for an hour or two of her querulous companions. Relieved, too, that in their own slightly muddled and certainly agitated state, neither Magpie nor Badger seemed to have taken any notice of the changes affecting herself: her listlessness, her newly lifeless hair, her darkening gown. As day wore on, Hannah felt less and less vivacious, as though her blood were drawing inward somehow, away from her extremities, pooling within her core. The breeze grew **stron**ger, fresher, and more redolent of sorcery.

Wandering the empty avenues of the ruined city, she came at length to a harbor. The cliff fell away in stages, forming a steep but passable staircase to the bay below, which was circular, surrounded by a broad beachhead, its sides curving in long, nearly symmetrical horns which almost touched. Stone buildings and paths covered slope and shore. The questing girl felt an uncanny certitude that Foxkith had passed this way—and equal certainty that he had remained upon the heights. The clear, deep waters of the bay below sparkled azure in the cool afternoon sun. Hannah turned away and continued eastward, across the interior of the isle.

She searched until dusk, at first through ruins. Later, leaving the wasted settlement, she continued through open countryside again. As before, she encountered hardly a blade of grass or a sprig of scrub, few animals, and those scrawny and circumspect. Attempts at conversation proved fruitless. Living things scurried off at the sight of her. On and on Hannah trudged as the heatless, brilliant sun declined, casting her ever-lengthening shadow before her across the stony, uneven ground. Rousing herself from her fog of fatigue, she realized belatedly that she had come too far to turn back now and meet the others at the square by dusk. Yet coming to a halt took effort. For the time being, she resolved to fare on.

At last the sun fell out of sight behind her to westward. Its light changed from pale butter to the faintest of yellow-greens, through golden honey into deep amber. She was near the far side of the isle. Somewhere before her lay the plateau's edge. The gentle rush and murmur of ocean reached her ears. She continued walking, nearly in a dream, the air around her rapidly cooling, sky changing from rose into wine and then dark, inky blue. Its light faded so rapidly she could scarce see her way. No moon rose. The scent of sorcery burned in her nostrils. Fireflies roved the air, tiny, bobbing glimmers against the gloom.

Something loomed before her. Hannah stopped short, blinking uncertainly. She realized with a start that it was a tree, a very great one—not overtall, but vastly spreading. The searching girl found herself beneath its canopy, standing among an immense network of roots that gripped the cliff hard beside the plateau's sheer drop-off to the sea below. She felt much higher here than at any time since having come ashore. The land must have lifted gradually, she suspected, until, now, beside this ancient tree, she stood upon the island's highest point.

Hannah stood reeling, a little dizzy. Her limbs seemed weighty as lead. She felt something yielding against her toes, a thing both warm and covered with dense, soft fur. Peering down through the darkening air, she saw nothing but two spots of light gleaming on two midnight-colored eyes. Wind stirred, bringing the rich, musk odor of foxes ever so slightly savored with the burnt tinge of sorcery. She whispered,

"Foxkith?" and felt his tongue slip lightly across her instep. Relief swept through her. She knelt laughing to fold him in her arms. Even hindered by distance, weariness and falling night, her heart had led her unerringly to him.

She lay down beside him in the dark, among the roots of the great, lone tree, grateful to be able at last to rest. She felt her voiceless beloved's thick, luxurious foxtail brush against her cheek as he nestled himself against her breast. She pillowed her head on one folded arm, gazing off into the blackness, watched stars winking between the swaying branches above. They were not quite barren, but rather waved sparsely in leaf. Gently, she stroked her mute companion, felt his whiskers tickling her cheek, his ribs swell and fall in a contented sigh. Her own heart lay troubled.

"Where is she, Foxkith?" she asked tiredly, near the end of her strength. "Why haven't we found the one we seek?" No answer. She had not expected one. She felt her eyelids closing, heavy as fishing weights. She could not have stayed wakeful a moment longer, had she tried. Hannah yawned, murmuring, "How long till we find her, my love? Where lies your Sorcerer Queen?"

Chapter 20
Ancient Mother

Soft rustling roused her. Hannah stirred, gazing about her at the blue gloom of first light. She sat among the roots of the vast tree standing at cliff's edge, its thick trunk twisted like a woman's swirling gown. A flat, barren space stretched away to the west, the direction from which she had come the evening before. Now, reclining beneath the tree, she looked up at its spreading boughs, enormous and gnarled with age, dipping low overhead. In the first faint glimmerings of dawn, the waking girl discerned a scant carpet of coppery foliage underneath, scattered among the roots between which she lay. It whispered in the slight, crisp wind.

Tired, a little foggy-headed still, Hannah stared harder through the gloom. Some of the fallen leaves around her were of oak, some aspen, others maple, hawthorn, and beech—yet she had seen but a single tree, this one alone, in her entire traverse of the isle. A few spindly fruits clung to the sparsely-leafed boughs above: sour apples and shriveled plums, speckled mandarins, withered peaches and pears. Scattered among them was a sprinkling of tiny tattered flowers: blighted may blossoms, frost-nipped cherry buds, pinched lime florets, and malformed olive blooms. Blinking, Hannah rubbed her eyes, uncertain whether she woke or dreamed.

With a start, she realized Foxkith no longer lay beside her—yet her lassitude made worry difficult to sustain. As soft susurrations continued all around, her disquiet faded into the background of her mind. She felt not drained exactly, but inward-turned, her energies conserving themselves rather than flowing forth. This for the first time in she knew not how long. The aroma of sorcery rose all around, as though respiring from the tree itself, from its earthen roots, its branches and bole, upward into the predawn sky. Gradually, she grew to understand that the sounds she heard were the gentle snap and rustle of fruit being plucked.

Turning with some effort against the strange resistance she felt in her limbs and neck, she beheld a pair of frail deer tugging figs from a limb not far from her. Straightening stiffly, she beheld three puny hares hunkered nearby, nibbling a pomegranate that had split upon the rocks. The sky lightened. She saw two young ounces, evidently lately wakened, arch and stretch, paces away on the other side of the trunk. Nearby, oblivious, a groundhog sat licking plum juice from his paws. Off to one side, a great, rilled chuckwalla hissed raucously, fending a scrawny polecat from his fallen mango.

"Gently, my children," whispered the tree. "My old limbs bear all too little. Parcel my yield, that it may last."

Hannah sat bolt upright. The animals near her all froze

or sprang away. The pilgrim girl stumbled to her feet, staring at the trunk of the tree. It bore the faint, unmistakable outline of a human figure. Even in this dimness before true dawn, she was able to discern it. Hannah gaped. The greenwood figure standing before her was silvery, tall, her body forming the great tree's bole. Above, branches reached and radiated like a myriad of up-stretched arms that mingled with and became her leafy hair. Smooth ridges of bark outlined the treewoman's venerable face. Below that, a dark and terrible hollow yawned in her breast as though, once lightning-rent, the wound had never closed.

"Who speaks?" Hannah stammered, her voice sharp with consternation.

At her words, the tree reared back creaking, as though caught in a strong wind. The wooden ridges delineating her face rearranged into an expression of surprise.

"A human voice?" the other began, her own a whispery echo of human speech. "How many years since last I heard—oh!"

The other seemed to catch sight of Hannah in the minimal light only now. Rigidly, with great difficulty, the tree leaned forward ever so slightly, as if to study her. "Child, how is it you've come here?"

The other's words were soft as rustling rushes. Hannah felt herself drawn, had to check herself from moving toward the other and her still, quiet voice.

"By boat," she answered carefully. "A miraculous craft made of silvery wood—like you."

The other's finely wrinkled face smiled. Ancient as she was, she was beautiful. Everything about the tree—her face, figure, even the scent of her—seemed curiously unstrange, and that lack of strangeness both uneased and attracted the outland girl who stood before her. Fear mingled with fascination in Hannah's breast.

"You're a brave lass," the one before her murmured, smiling still. Hannah glanced away. She did not feel brave. "Time was even the stoutest feared trespass on Faraway Isle."

The fair-haired girl looked up, taken by surprise. "Faraway?" she asked, not certain she had heard it right. "Is that the name of this place?"

The other nodded. Hannah shook herself, amazed. How often had she heard cottars speak the island's name, and just as often misunderstood? The tree loomed closer, her aged expression attentive, interested, and not at all unkind.

"What brings you here?"

"A . . . friend," Hannah answered, remembering caution now. She studied the one before her in the growing light uncertainly. "But what are you? I've never before heard speech from a tree."

The other laughed, very delicately, her many branches tossing, quivering with mirth. "Is that what you take me for?" she whispered. "Well, in a way, I suppose I am— though my followers have long called me Ancient Mother, and once, long before that, Matron—and even Maiden at the dawn of my day."

Echoes of memory stirred in Hannah, and with them a tentative understanding. "You're the one whom the holyfolk spoke of!" she exclaimed. *The one they and the reapers mistook me for,* she added silently. And the girls doing laundry among the reeds. Aloud, she said, "The one who embodies Mother, Matron, and Maiden in one."

Fractionally, the other nodded. All her movements were measured, as though they took great will to accomplish. New comprehension broke over Hannah. "You're the one whose story I saw embroidered," she blurted out. "In Marda's cottage: upon an isle, a wounded tree . . . and a man, sailing away."

The wayfarer stopped herself. Though beautifully stitched, the tale upon the coverlet had both frightened and saddened her. Still smiling faintly, the treewoman sighed.

"So folk on the mainland remember me yet—the holy-folk, at any rate. That's well." Her expression clouded. The silvery wood of her brows drew together. "Do the common folk no longer hold me in memory?"

Hannah felt herself begin to flush.

"You mustn't mistake my ignorance for the common run," she muttered, abashed. "Until but a few moons ago, I lived fast in a Tanglewood. My keeper told me nothing of the world beyond."

Again, she stopped herself. Had she said too much? Who was this fabulous fruiting, flowering wight? Dared Hannah trust her? She seemed honest, peaceable, and kind—yet, the Wizard, too, had once seemed kind. The runaway girl shifted nervously, hoping the other would pay her words no particular heed, let what she had just said pass without comment. The treewoman's expression, however, remained troubled.

"Nothing?" she whispered. "Did he tell you nothing at all? That was cruel. . . . !"

The sun, not yet visible, had floated closer to horizon's edge. Its crimson light infused the sky all shades of melon, nectarine, and peach. A glimmer upon the Ancient Mother's breast told Hannah that sap was oozing from the deep-riven cleft: an old wound, bleeding still. Anxious to change the subject, Hannah broke in.

"Will you speak of yourself?" she asked. "Tell me the meaning of the tale on Marda's coverlet—how you came by that scar."

Now the other groaned, an inner creaking like wood ready to give way—and for a moment, Hannah felt a stab of apprehension. But the great tree quieted, shaking her head just barely. Above, her many branches whispered and swayed.

"Where to begin, child? Where to begin?" All around them, the animals had quietly, unobtrusively, returned to foraging. The other's gaze found hers. "Describe the scene on this coverlet. It contained a man, you say. What manner of man?"

Hannah thought a moment. "A fair-haired man in a boat. He held a blade in one hand, and in the other, a flowering sprig."

"And when you looked on the image of this man," the other asked, "did it remind you of anyone?"

The woodland girl stopped short. The treewoman's eyes, weary and kindly, gazed into hers. Hannah stood rooted. Listening to the soft words, like wind among the leaves, she felt a growing chill.

"The Wizard!" she burst out suddenly, only just now aware, for the first time. "He looked like the Master of the Wood—"

Hannah began to shake. The Ancient Mother took no notice. Ever so slightly, she nodded, her branches gently tossing.

"And so it was he, though in younger days, before he gained the Tanglewood. The scene you describe pictured him sailing away from this island, bearing the priceless prize he stole from me and the means he used to do so."

The Ancient Mother rose before her. Hannah stood trembling. "The Wizard, my master . . . he came from here?"

"Born here," the great tree replied. "Long ago, when my servitors were human beings."

"I . . . saw the ruins of a city," the traveler girl managed, unnerved. Her teeth chattered. She longed for Foxkith's arms. "Ships, a tabernacle—a palace?—and the harbor below."

"Indeed," the woodland goddess nodded. "In that tabernacle, my followers sang praises and offered prayers. From that harbor, they traded with all the world. In that palace dwelt my priestesses and this island's philosopher-kings with their many sons who served me. Your Wizard was one such, foremost among the King's heirs. He sailed to sea as a young man and remained away in the world long years. What evil seized him there, I can only guess. His heart was hidden from me, though I loved him dear."

Hannah stood, thoughts in a roil, hugging herself against the chill, impending dawn and the shock of learning so unexpectedly that the Wizard who had imprisoned her and the younger man depicted on the old needlewoman's quilt were one and the same. Hannah struggled to quiet her turmoil, still the frantic beating of her pulse. The ancient treewoman rambled on. The girl found the soft, wistful voice soothing, almost hypnotic. It was a mercy for a little space just to listen, not to have to think.

"I'd fostered him among his many brothers, thinking that in time it would be he whom I'd name to succeed his sire. But he sailed away and remained away. His father died. Still he didn't return. I dispatched messengers to the four winds in search of him, but he couldn't be found. I feared he'd perished, and blamed myself, my inattention. I'd indulged him, let him alone, failed to curb his reckless ambition to gain by sorcery all the knowledge of the world—convinced he would soon see his folly, abandon it, and return to me. But he did not return."

The beldame cast her old eyes seaward, held them there a long moment, sadly, as though awaiting her wayward favorite still. The silence stretched so long, it seemed she was done. Hannah chafed her arms, unable to get warm. Then heavily, the other sighed and, to the woodland girl's surprise, picked up her story's thread.

"I appointed one of his brothers in his place, a fine man, ever just and fair, with coal-black hair and laughing eyes."

Hannah thought of Foxkith, smiling upon the strand, his hair lifted by the breeze. As the treewoman described her island's long-ago king, it was Foxkith's face that Hannah saw.

"He ruled wisely, and sired many, many sons. Under his stewardship, our peaceful isle prospered as never before. I came to see the wisdom of my choice, for he proved a steadier, far more prudent king than ever my wayfarer would have been. His youngest son became my darling in turn, very like his father. This new crop of philosopher-princes I fostered with tender care, as I had so many generations before them.

Yet always in the back of my mind, I awaited my prodigal's return—unable to give him up for dead."

Another meditative silence. Hannah stood fidgeting, torn: reluctant to prod, yet at the same time chafing to hear the origin of her former master and his Wood—and with it, perhaps, her own origin as well. The animals moved quietly through the cold, bleak dawn, ignoring Hannah now as they might a bit of driftwood or a withe. At last the treewoman stirred. Hannah's heart quickened.

"Then one day, out of the mist, he returned, sailing back into the harbor in a ghostly craft such as I'd thought only my magical priestesses knew how to conjure. What a welcome my people gave him! How warmly his old friends embraced him. My wanderer seemed to return their friendship, without jealousy at another's now holding the honor he had himself once expected to assume. Now his brother held the post, and had for years, with many daughters serving in my tabernacle and many sons who might one day succeed him. My wanderer hadn't a one. Yet he pretended happiness for his brother's high estate, saluted his nieces and nephews.

"But he did not come to me. I made excuses to myself, sensing the change in him, even here, far removed from the city as I am. My priestesses brought word to me, and my vision then was clear and strong. I was far too proud to send for him. And he kept himself hidden from my view, wrapped in a faint murk. Nothing extravagant enough to rouse my suspicions, just barely sufficient to keep me from reading his inmost heart. There, deep within himself, he harbored a secret intent."

Again the Ancient Mother sighed, bitterly this time. Hannah found the chill in her blood abating somewhat. As quietly as she could, she seated herself once more among the roots, hugging her knees, listening to the other's tale.

"My first hint of danger came when I learned of his scheme to control our island's trade. As all before him had, his brother the King supported our age-old custom of setting fair price for well-made goods. My wanderer urged him to mandate bargaining for more. Our goods were unique, he said, the mainlanders able to pay far more than we asked. Our isle could grow rich, he said. The King looked at him. 'Brother,' he said, 'we're already rich. Rich in our work, in our children, in our homes. Gold we use only for exchange and ornament. Why hoard it?'"

Hannah sat in the treewoman's shadow. The tang of basil and bitter herbs filled the air around her. The tree herself was the source, the woodland girl felt sure. Were her words sorcerous? Why did Hannah herself feel so listless in the other's presence—captivated and yet completely safe? The goddess went on.

"Troubled, the King came to me and spoke of these words the two of them had exchanged. I resolved to summon my wanderer then, and learn his heart. He came willingly enough. Speaking with him here alone, my priestesses beyond earshot, I learned many things. Though he pretended humility—made abject apology for his failure to visit me, pleading the press of affairs, the many friends and relations he must greet and once more come to know—I sensed duplicity."

Hannah breathed deep, trying to clear her head. The lassitude that had been stealing over her since she had come to this isle continued its inexorable progress. She felt weary to the bone, her limbs strangely wooden and stiff. Despite her full night's rest, having once more sunk down, she felt she might not be able to rise. Deeply absorbed in the telling, her hostess continued, seeming to take no note of her young guest's distress.

"Truth to tell, I now think he'd been sniffing the nobles out, to see who among them were disaffected and could be persuaded to revolt. Finding all loyal to the King, he must have been disappointed—but not daunted. So great was his desire for gold, he'd stop at nothing to accumulate more. My priestesses had discovered since his return that he'd brought heaps of it, hoping to bribe my officials. It had all been wasted. None took the bribe."

The great tree moved in the wind, sighing. Despite her eagerness, Hannah forced herself to hold her tongue. It seemed the other had stood silent so long that now she must tell her tale out to its end, without interruption, only a pause now and again for breath.

"When I revealed that I knew of his attempts to buy influence, he prevaricated in alarm. Customs differed on the mainland, he said. He'd lived long among those folk, unwittingly adopted their ways. He'd forgotten bribes were forbidden here, indeed nearly unheard of. If I couldn't excuse his error, he would be devastated. The confession seemed wrenched from him, heartfelt. I was sorely tempted to forgive all, forget his misdeeds—yet still I sensed withholding, lies.

"I asked him what knowledge he'd found upon the mainland. He spoke of this or that minor art: the lighting of fire with a fingersnap; changing a herringbone into a comb, or a moth into a pearl; the whistling of a broom—arts my healwomen had all learned in childhood. Even some of my fosterlings, those that had a bit of magic in their blood. But he spoke of these charms as though they were weighty feats: deliberately so. I suspect he hoped to throw me from the scent, convince me his powers were puny.

"But all about him, the air roiled redolent of sorcery, blatant now, unconcealable. I'd no doubt at all that in the years he'd been away, he'd studied feverishly to become a wizard of formidable power. So I asked specifically after his gold. He seemed near panic. Clearly he'd thought his powers enough to shield it from all eyes, even mine. I told him the precise extent of his hidden hoard and inquired how he'd come by it. Unprepared, he stammered something of trade.

"What trade?" I replied. "You left this isle with next to nothing and have never returned till now. Do you think that because I spurn lucre, I'm ignorant of its use? What did you trade for all this gold?"

"And at last he could only admit it had been sorcery. Magical favors. Cures for a price. Secrets. Power. He'd sold them all for coin and jewels, a terrible outrage, mocking our law. A magicker's gifts must be shared freely, as has always been our way. It's to receive guidance in these matters that my attendants are all selected as children and raised in the tabernacle where their talents can be strengthened and trained. Like some careless wastrel, my wanderer had debased the riches of his folk for his own greed."

It seemed the treewoman's shadow darkened. Hannah felt it lancing through her like a sword. She dared not move, dared not breath a word lest she break the other's spell and end her tale too soon. The ancient tree seemed to lean away from her, racked with a pain barely expressible. Her words were clipped.

"What dismay I felt at his betrayal! I considered banishing him, but realized that to do so would simply foist him back upon the world. Should I order him stripped of his ill-gotten wealth, that he might make no more mischief among my nobles? Yes, of course, at the very least. But what of his sorcery? At last I resolved to do what should have been done long past: he must enter the service of the tabernacle, where his overweening ambition could be tempered, his magical bent harnessed to succor and to heal."

Standing nearly motionless, backlit by the still-hidden sun, the Ancient Mother fell once more into brooding silence. Wind stirred. The dawn air freshened. The sea washed far, far beyond the precipice's edge. Like the pilgrims in the hall at Linnel, Hannah waited, tense and expectant, for the other to resume.

"Hearing my pronouncement, he became half-crazed. For one wild moment, I feared he meant to fling himself over the cliff's edge into the sea. At the last instant, however, he reconsidered, realizing that in death lay only defeat. Though he could not immediately escape my sentence, he meant to triumph in time. Flight was useless, for my priestesses, hearing our raised voices, had hurried closer, prepared to use their powers if he should refuse to surrender peaceably. No sorcerous craft could spirit him away quickly enough to escape them—no corner of the world could hide him from my sight, were I truly determined to find him."

The treewoman's tone grew hard.

"At last, his stubbornness seemed broken. He collapsed

in tears, begging forgiveness for his arrogance, offering his ill-gotten wealth for the benefit of the isle and promising to serve faithfully, using his skills only for good without thought of reward. I bade my healwomen take him directly to the tabernacle and send for the King, whom I told only that his brother wished to withdraw from public life and dedicate himself to priestly service. Though puzzled by the suddenness of his brother's decision, the King nevertheless expressed relief. His brother had seemed much troubled of late. A period of quiet contemplation would surely do him good."

The voice of the tree abruptly softened, her gaze cast down, her fragile branches drooping as though beneath a burden nearly too great to bear. Hannah watched, waited—weary, yet on edge.

"How deeply now do I regret not confiding in my loyal King," the Ancient Mother breathed. "How foolish of me, and how vain my wish to protect—still!—my untrustworthy favorite. I wanted no one to know of his errors save me, and that was my undoing. Outwardly penitent, he entered the tabernacle and there remained three years, quietly going about his duties, his crushed humility plain for all to see. Even I grew complacent, proud of my success, his obvious reform. I should have known! All the while, under cover of night, he was rifling the great library of the tabernacle, searching for knowledge, power, vengeance to ruin this isle and all its denizens. Hunting a spell whereby he might one day regain his lost gold and infinitely more besides. Seeking a weapon with which to destroy me."

Chapter 21
Thief

The stately woman within the tree paused in her narrative, her silvery face gone ashen with memory. Hannah sensed dawn just on the verge of breaking, the gray sky growing ever more luminous. The silent creatures all around—blind moles and hump-shelled tortoises, scrawny rock hens and ring-tailed foragers—had stopped their browsing now, grown still, listening. Clearly they understood their provider's speech. Wind stirred and sighed. The crash of surf on the rocky shore below reached Hannah's ears, now faint, now forcefully. The Ancient Mother closed her eyes. Her tone dropped lower yet. Seated before her, among her roots, the listening girl had to lean closer to catch her words.

"In time, my pretended penitent achieved his vengeful goal. Within the tabernacle's most sacred texts, he came across the secret of my power—all the vast enchantment that then I held, of which but dim shadows now remain."

The treewoman laughed ruefully, incongruously, her worn visage deeply lined with pain. Hannah took in every word.

"Child, once I could gaze from here to the other side of the world, far across the sea to the mainland shore, and inland, to the farthest corners of the globe. Rains fell at my nod. Winds blew to my sigh. My changing raiment spun the seasons round. The heavens turned, and the sun, moon, and stars danced to the rhythm of my beating heart. Within me lay the key to my magical power: the life-green sap that coursed through me from my deep-set roots, permeating my heartwood, sweetening my fruit, and respiring from my leaves in numinous wafts."

Hannah found herself nodding. A feeling of kinship, of connection, overwhelmed her suddenly. She could not say why.

"Because of this, the sick have always been brought to me, to consume my fruit, inhale my breath, recline among my ancient roots, and find healing. My heart's blood was then the lifeforce of the world, the generation and the mending of all things—once, once. . . . And I gave it freely to all who asked, refusing recompense. Yet when first I'd proffered my embrace to heal my wanderer's greed, he'd declined the kiss, with many groans and tears. He called himself unworthy, promised to partake in time, but only after he'd abased himself and made amends. I wouldn't force him."

Sadly, she shook her head, all her branches trembling at the subtle motion. Copper-colored leaves, like little flames, fluttered around Hannah in the cool air. The treewoman sighed.

"His false repentance won my trust, bought time enough

for him to discover a means to overcome me and steal—for his own base uses—my natural powers. For though I'm ancient past counting, and some call me Mother-Goddess to the world, I'm not all-knowing. What little wisdom I own's been hard-won, and still I live and age and learn. In three years' time, my prodigal pronounced himself cleansed, his penance at end. He proclaimed himself ready to reconcile with me and return to public life as a physician among his family and friends. In addition to the holy kiss of peace, he wished to present me with a gift made by his own hands, a humble token of his gratitude for my perceiving his calamitous course and diverting him in time. His brother the King declared a feast day in rejoicing."

Again, silence. No sound for many heartbeats but the wash of waves far, far below, the rustling of leaves and quiet shifting among the animals. Almost as if unable to move, Hannah waited. Wistfully, the Ancient Mother spoke.

"A great procession brought my traitor to me from the temple. Here before the King and all his kith—before the nobles, my priestesses and healwomen, before the merchant folk, indeed all the people of the isle—my beloved pretender lamented his many unnamed faults. He vowed lifelong reparation, in token of which he'd fashioned a gift, forged in the tabernacle in secret—though with the permission of my chief priestess. I'd instructed her to supply him with whatever materials he should request and refrain from spying. She was to allow him to work in perfect privacy, so sure was I of his sincerity. Nor did I myself stoop even once to observe him about his labors.

"My trust—or was it pride?—proved my undoing. Not

the slightest prick of doubt thrilled me as my wanderer unveiled the implement he'd made. Wrought of mingled gold and silver, copper and bronze, the great hooked blade gleamed. Figures covered it: huntsmen pursuing their prey, sea creatures struggling and drowning in nets, birds beating against the bars of tiny, ornate cages. Frightful scenes, and yet so cunningly contrived. All made by sorcery, I saw—yet even that didn't warn me. His last feat, I told myself, his final deed of frivolous conjuring before renouncing such vanities to devote himself entirely to the healing arts. All smiles, as though at once proud and shy of others' appraisal, he held it up. Intrigued, I bent down to examine it.

"'What is it?' I asked at last, the first hint of unease beginning to stir within my breast. 'A sword? Would you pledge peace with a sword?'

"A laugh escaped him, quickly bitten off.

"'No, Lady,' he answered softly, though I sensed bridled brashness beneath the humble tone. I bent nearer yet. 'A pruning hook,' he whispered, 'such as orchardmen use. Our isle's renowned for its yield: figs and olives, apples, citrons, almonds and quince. The orchardmen of Faraway use such tools as this to tend their groves and pluck down the sweet fruits of their toil—as I mean to do. Closer, hag. I'll trim you to a size more to my liking and seize what lends you all your power!'

"The words hissed out in such a rush that in that first heartbeat, I didn't comprehend. I stood aghast, staring at the one I'd so unwisely adored, so long preferred above any other, once showered with privileges that had only spoiled him out of all honor, all modesty and restraint. In that same instant, he lunged, lancing the terrible blade across my breast, cleaving me here, where the wound still bleeds. Lightning hurled from a cloudless sky could not have stunned me more.

"Then he had it, the thing he'd come to steal, the sacred bud sprouting from my breast, sprung from my sapwood and green heart's blood, the well of my strength and hub of my powers—gashed out of me now in a splintering wrench. I screamed, or groaned, my strength fast ebbing, life bleeding from me in a rush as he held the severed floret high, laughing like one crazed with merciless triumph, drunk on his own greed now satisfied, infused with what had moments before been my power—his now, or in his possession at least.

"The earth shook. Thunder pealed. Far in the distance across the isle, I heard columns falling, stone walls shattering, roofs caving in. The great crowd around me—the entire population of the isle—cried out in terror. Still laughing, he turned to face them. Slowly, almost contemptuously, he lowered the blade. It had completed its task. Its part in his ruse was done. Instead, with a lazy flourish, he brandished aloft his stolen wand. My priestesses were dashed to the earth before him, my King and courtiers slammed to their knees with its power."

Her tone filled with grief, horror, guilt, and regret. Hannah dared not breathe a word. The Ancient Mother's voice murmured on, unstoppable as the tide.

"This isle keeps no standing army and never has, only a company of the King's ceremonial guard, who serve as escorts to the royal family or others embarked abroad on business of state. These brave knights rushed forward, only to be repelled by another blast, as were the merchants and common folk also surging to my aid. He felled them all: some lying dazed, some writhing in agony, but none dead. Even this he'd planned. He wanted us alive—me in particular—to acknowledge his mastery.

Her words grew even more bitter. Hannah listened, hushed. The spurned goddess cast down her eyes.

"My wound had very nearly drained me, but this much I recall: gleefully, my attacker swept his budding rod once more in the direction of my loyal followers. Instantly, they began to change, some into cats or hares, brown bats, bears; raccoons and snakes, oxen, owls; loons, drakes, other fowls; lynx, deer, river minks—so many I cannot name them all in their variety. I saw my chief priestess transformed into a heron, heard her mournful cry as she flew away. The King himself became a coal-black wolf; his youngest son a fox, the other children all manner of beasts: new-fletched eagles, a lion's cub, a red roan colt, a ginger bear, a gamecock, a half-grown brindled bull. All transformed in the space of a breath and all staggered, wildered by the suddenness, the enormity of the change.

"Most scattered, keening and bawling with fear, a mad flight of animals scrambling in all directions. Only the King seemed to have kept some remainder of his wits. With an anguished howl, he sprang at my attacker—and paid with his life. His brother struck him down, not with the wand but with the blade. He dealt the blow almost casually, as though not deigning to use wizardry, preferring that his rival's death be directly and undeniably the work of his own hand. At last, when all my transmogrified courtiers had fled, he turned to me.

"'Bleed, crone,' he snarled. 'Seep till the end of time. I won't finish you, nor can you restore yourself without the magic I've claimed from you—mine now by right of conquest. Soon I'll depart this isle. Once on the mainland, I'll teach the world to fear me, nor rest till all its wealth be mine. Mull that, monstress, and may you be a long time dying.'

"I saw him no more. He fled the isle, his sorcerous craft laden with stolen gold, all the fair trinkets of Faraway, robbed from the tabernacle and the public coffers, along with that he had himself once brought to the isle. After, for some unimaginable period of time, I knew nothing more, too badly damaged even to sense the world around me. What woke me at last, after I know not how vast a span, was my followers, all in animal shape, crowding about as though to give me succor. Drawn by half-memories, perhaps. I feel sure some recalled certain fragments of their past. They can speak, you know, but seldom do. Many, I fear, lost their wits entirely.

"They were starving, having eaten every scrap of food upon the isle except each other. Even the carnivores, I sensed, hunted only the true animals of the isle, never those who'd once been human like themselves. The bleeding of my sap had slowed, the air grown infinitely colder. Without my former power to turn the seasons, the world had settled into raw and endless winter, forever unchanging now. Few growing things could fight the constant cold enough to sprout, to flower, fruit, and seed. The Wizard must have been consuming all my stolen magic for himself—though I doubt he knew how properly to use it. My sight, so greatly dimmed now by infirmity, managed to glimpse him only once, deep in a tangled wood, extorting gold and jewels from rulers far and commoners near."

Again a span of silence, so long that at first the stranger girl half-feared the Ancient Mother had ended her tale, too burdened now with exhaustion or grief. But at last she stirred, strove valiantly to continue. Her weakened voice seemed but a breath upon the breeze.

"But what of my budding branch, I wondered? Where lay my kidnapped strength? It lived on, I knew. Were it ever to die, the Wizard would immediately lose his vigor. He must be preserving the precious sprig somehow, nurturing it, or at least allowing it to grow. I resolved to fight off despair. Fettered as I was, I sought means to rescue my stolen slip. Rooted, wounded, barely alive, I'd watched helpless as this Wizard wielded his purloined powers to cast my people into beasts, confuse their wits, plunder their stores. And for years after, my loving folk—beasts though they were—had tended me as best they might, taking as little of my poor fruit as they dared to keep themselves alive.

"Bit by bit, I managed to rally, hoarding my strength by dropfuls until I'd gathered enough to change one of my young princelings back to his true human shape. Singly, sometimes in pairs, or even trios, over many years, I disenchanted them. Even though ages had passed, your Wizard's transformation had not only frozen my folk as beasts, but trapped them in time as well. They remained ageless while in animal shape. Those who'd been children remained young. Those who'd been old aged no further until I broke their spell. But the cost for me of each such effort was dreadful debilitation. Each time I effected the change, I swooned deeply into myself, utterly drained and unable to rouse for uncounted moons.

"Those fosterlings I was able to restore to humanity retained only the dimmest memories. As in a dream, they wandered to the shore, where they found my ghostly craft to bear them to the mainland. There they fashioned armor, earned steeds, and set out, the only thoughts in their clouded minds of the quest to which I'd set them: find the Wizard in his Tanglewood and recover the treasure he'd stolen from me. No word, no deed, must turn them from the task, for only if one of these knights-errant succeeded could he hope to restore those left behind to their rightful shape, heal my great injury and with it, the world—to say nothing of recovering his own wits, his own memory and name."

Hannah's limbs prickled, though whether with cold, or long sitting, she was not sure. Despite herself, her gaze strayed to the treewoman's breast. Wind whistled through the hollow there. No streaming sap could ever hope to fill that chasm. Her countless limbs tossed and rustled overhead. Day had well and truly broken at last, the sky glorious amber, the coppery sun just peering above horizon's edge.

Faintly at first, then drawing rapidly nearer, a commotion to westward reached the ears of the waiting girl. Turning, she saw black, vulpine Foxkith dashing across the rocky open space, followed by the red foxlets, Magpie winging with a will, and even Badger far in the distance, puffing after them. Hannah struggled to her feet as Foxkith bounded to stand on toes and give her hand a quick swipe before whirling to crouch in front of the treewoman, head up, ears cocked. Slowly—yet with more speed than Hannah had yet seen her muster—the tree straightened, creaking, as though seized with surprise.

"Foxkith!" she exclaimed. "But what's this? I sent you forth a man. How is it you've become a fox again?"

Hannah caught in her breath. "How do you know that name?" she demanded. "That's my name for him. I named him so when he couldn't remember his own true name."

The greenwood figure before her began to quake. After such a long and harrowing tale, the reaction was so unexpected it took the wayward girl moments to realize that it was laughter shaking the other's form: a sudden, joyous mirth, the sound of which was like fresh, clear water hurrying over stones.

"Would I not know my own fosterling," the Ancient Mother replied, "and the fine true name he's borne since birth? It's the same fine, forgotten name I've held safe for him this twelvemonth, since I sent him forth to face your Wizard and win back the world."

Hannah bit her tongue. The tree gazed tenderly down upon her and the swart fox at her side. Surprise and delight lit those weary eyes. The woodland girl felt her skin draw taut, the blood within her cool and shrink. All on a sudden, her thoughts cleared. The strange feeling of lassitude evaporated. For the first time, she allowed herself to apprehend exactly who and what it was that rose before her, in whose shadow she now found herself. Hannah took a step back, a little dismayed, fully aware at last that she stood in the presence not only of the triune goddess of pilgrims and holyfolk, but also of her truelove's Sorcerer Queen.

Chapter 22
Russet Hannah

"You're she," Hannah breathed. "Foxkith's foster mother. The Sorcerer Queen!"

The treewoman shrugged ever so slightly, her kindly expression grown puzzled now. "Whyever do you call me such a thing?" she mused. "That's never been among my names."

The girl before her hesitated. "It was Foxkith's term for you—or rather, mine from his description of you."

The other chuckled, at once grandly amused and sadly irked. "Was that all he could recall," she murmured, "to think me some mere sorcerer?"

"He called you Queen of the isle," Hannah hastily amended, "and told me he loved you dear, that you'd fostered him. He was ready to die for you, and nearly did so of the wounds he'd taken from the Golden Boar."

The Ancient Mother swayed as in a gentle breeze, though no wind now stirred. "A boar—is this the shape my thief now wears?"

Hannah nodded, teeth clenched. "A murderous boar that eats human flesh."

If the wooden goddess could have wept, the woodland girl realized, she would have done so then, gazing off at nothing, her face drawn, figure totally still. But she said only, "Then he must pay the price."

Hannah hesitated, not quite certain what the other meant. She had spoken reflectively, as to herself, and seemed to require no reply. Foxkith crouched before her still, attentive, mute. Above him, Magpie swooped through the air to come to rest on one of the branches near the Mother's wizened face. The treewoman glanced up at her.

"Ah," she said, as if scarce surprised. "You've been away a rare long time. Do you recall me any better than Foxkith?"

For once, the pied bird neither clucked nor cawed, fluttered nor fussed, but dipped respectfully low upon her perch. "Yes, Lady," she whispered, as though overawed. "I do remember now."

The foxlets arrived in a swirl of yapping and boisterous play. They barged tumbling about the treewoman's roots.

"Bark, bole, root, tree!" they clamored, biting playfully at Foxkith, trying to bully him into joining their game. The black fox forbore them gracefully. The Ancient Mother managed a faint chuckle.

"Here you are, children, come back to me at last. And you!" She turned to Badger just waddling near. "How long have my city's gardens lain untended in your absence?" Her chiding was gentle, brimful of affection and joy, her grief of a few moments before seemingly forgotten.

"Too long, Lady," the old brock puffed, dipping his nose to the ground. "I, too, now recollect—though I doubt these silly whippersnappers do." He nodded in some annoyance at the fox pups, who continued their nipping, tumbling game, oblivious to who or what they discombobulated.

"Peace," the treewoman urged. "Let them play."

Badger bowed his head. The risen sun had come into full glory now, casting warm, ruddy light through the cool, blue air. The foxlets' tussling grew so vigorous that Hannah had to step aside. Once free of the treewoman's shadow, she stood in the streaming sun. Behind her, the Ancient Mother drew breath sharply, almost a gasp. The pilgrim girl turned to find the other staring at her as though just now, for the first time having caught clear sight of her.

"Oh," whispered the ancient tree. "O child, what are you?"

A frenzy of startled barking from the fox pups. As Hannah fell back farther, Foxkith darted to her, tugging the hem of her garment to draw her once more closer to the tree. The Ancient Mother peered at her. Before her, the runaway girl stood bewildered, unsure quite how to answer the other's query.

"My name is Hannah," she said at last. "Once Brown Hannah, then Green. Lately I've found myself Golden."

"Hannah," murmured the woman in the tree. Her lined face shone in mingled wonder and delight. "What a lovely name. But why call yourself brown, or green, or even golden, my dear, when you're so clearly russet?"

Puzzled, Hannah glanced down at her discolored gown—and realized with a start, that it had once more entirely changed hue. By the ember-colored light of dawn, it was rusty as redwood, a gorgeous, bright pigment more vivid than any it had ever borne.

"What's this?" Hannah gasped, fingering the gauzy, translucent tissue, which felt crisper than before, softly crackling, like corn husks. Her fingers looked reddish through the stuff. "Why does my gown keep transforming?"

Before her, the treewoman nodded. "The season turns. I feel it now: autumn! Small wonder, your change of gown."

Hannah scarcely heard her. Her head felt odd. Putting one hand to her temple, she started anew, recognizing that her hair, too, had altered. Overnight the shabby straw and spent seedcorn previously sprouting there had vanished. Instead, her tresses now hung full of amber acorns and speckled silkweed pods. Flame-bright clouds of lacy seeds streamed from her, lifted by the morning wind. The savor and season of the air all around her felt keener than it had, poppy-hued sun welcomely warm in the tangy air. She could no longer distinguish the treewoman's strong, spice-tinged scent from her own.

"Why does what grows in my hair keep shifting?" she muttered. "When first I came to this isle, I felt faded, worn. . . ."

Almost imperceptibly, the other nodded. "I remember feeling so myself," she answered fondly. "Just before each change: Winter Damsel into Spring Maid, Spring Maid into Summer Girl, Summer Girl to Autumn Lass, and on and on. Pay it no mind. It passes."

Hannah shook her head. Many more creatures clustered about them now than she had noticed before: woodchucks and wildcats, cockerels and shrews. They seemed to be taking new interest in Hannah, crowding closer than they had, eyeing her intently, almost speculatively, noses twitching in the breeze. Black Foxkith lolled panting among the great tree's knotted roots, completely unconcerned.

"But the animals," Hannah insisted. "They scarcely took note of me yesterday. Now I'm changed, and they do. I feel different. Better, but—"

The Ancient Mother sobered. "But let us not speak of these matters just yet." Her voice was both gentle and firm. Her branches stirred in the lifting wind. "Tell me of Foxkith. Surely you came less to learn of yourself than to succor him? How is it he comes before me now in fox's shape, when I sent him forth a man?"

Hannah wrung her hands, her own plight instantly forgotten. "The Wizard changed him. If . . . if I tell you where the treasure lies, will you restore him?"

She was unable to keep the note of desperation from her voice. Foxkith's foster mother was her only hope. Before her, the Sorcerer Queen made no direct reply. Instead, she bade her, "Soft. Speak of your Wizard, of your dealings with him, and Foxkith's. How did you come to escape his hold?"

Frustrated, Hannah spoke in a rush. "I dwelt more years than I can recall in the Wizard's Wood. Flowers sprouted in my hair, but every moon, I plucked them out to brew a draught for him to drink."

A shadow crossed the ancient's face, brows knit, lips pursed in motherly concern. Impatient, the fair girl hurried on.

"Young knights came, time and again. Always they were slain. . . ."

The other's groan interrupted her. "Ah, I knew that," the treewoman sighed. "Knew, for they didn't return. Knew, though I no longer see beyond the world's end, perceive little farther than my own roots now. Knew, but dared to hope. Not slain! All my fosterlings. . . ."

Trembling racked her. Hannah could think of no comfort she might lend. She, too, had wept for the knights, unable to save them.

"The Wizard himself slew them," she said quietly, "taking the form of a great Golden Boar."

The other nodded. So much she had already learned.

"In that guise," Hannah continued, "he stalked the countryside, extorting a merciless tax from starving cottars to add to his treasure hoard."

She saw the Ancient Mother wince, her gaze cast down, as though finding Hannah's words too grievous to bear. Uncertainly, the russet-clad girl waited. At last the other bade her, "Go on."

"I learned these things shortly before Foxkith came. When I saw him making for the Wood, I tried to warn him. But he wouldn't be turned, only took a lily from my hair to wear upon his breast."

Without thinking, she reached one hand to her locks, but found no flowers there, only coppery crabapple buds and tiny, velvet apricots.

"I found him later," Hannah said, "badly wounded but not killed. My bloom had saved him somehow; the Boar feared it. I hid Foxkith in a thicket of thorns and mended him, bringing the Wizard only meager draughts."

Unobtrusively, without seeming to move, the animals were

drawing nearer. Hannah turned away, ignoring them, urgent to convey her story to the island goddess.

"My gown turned green; my hair began to flower in earnest. Foxkith could tell me but little of his home, of his life before. I feared fever'd muddled him."

She glanced at her young knight, trapped now in fox's shape, lounging among the sprawling roots of the sorcerous tree, grinning his foxy grin. She forced herself on.

"He mended. I tried to send him to safety, but he wouldn't go. Instead he followed me into the heart of the Wood to confront the Wizard, who foxed and silenced him."

Hannah's voice shook, remembering.

"I penned the Wizard, using charms I never knew I had. A hedge of thorns sprang up around him. There he remains imprisoned to this day, sometimes in human shape, sometimes a boar. No matter. He's too weakened to break free."

Hannah paused for breath, her voice growing tight. The silent, ever-increasing press of animals about her reminded her eerily of pilgrims crowding the great tabernacle in Linnel. She shut them out of her mind.

"I took Foxkith and Magpie, Badger and the fox pups with me and fled. We wandered long. My gown turned yellow. No soul we met had ever heard of the Sorcerer Queen— as I called you then."

Her eyes found those of the Ancient Mother.

"But I've found you now, in spite of all. If I return to you the Wizard's treasure, will you restore my friend to human shape?"

"Treasure," the other whispered, seemingly taken aback. "Do you mean his hoard?"

The woodland girl nodded vigorously. "Great heaps, piled higher than my head: coin, jewels, silver cups. Arms and armor, burnished plates . . ."

"O Hannah." The other with infinite sadness sighed. "Have you comprehended nothing? What use have I for glittering things? It's the Wizard's wand that is the treasure, not his gold."

Hannah felt her heart begin to beat in her throat. She glanced at Foxkith, who watched her, panting; at Magpie perched in the branches above; at Badger among the roots below, and the foxlets, who had at last left off their play, sprawled licking their paws. The other wildered birds and beasts skulked tentatively about, watching silently, no longer making even a pretense of foraging. Surely they listened. How much, she wondered, did they understand? Swallowing hard, the russet-robed girl addressed the tree.

"Wand?" she asked, her voice thin and hoarse. "He holds no wand. Has never wielded one. All his magic came from himself: his eyes, his hands—and it's ebbed. Ebbed too far. He can't change Foxkith back now, even if he wished."

The Ancient Mother listened gravely. Hannah felt herself growing frantic.

"But surely *you* can. You've done so before. You've told me! I'll give you anything—all I own. Anything within my power. Ask! What must you have to turn him back?"

Ever so gently, the other sighed, a wistful sound like the pattering of leaves.

"Once, when I was young," she breathed, "before my bud was rent from me, I could have done so without a thought. But I'm ancient now, and much diminished. My powers fail—further with each passing moon. These days it's all I can muster simply to produce fruit enough to feed this poor ensorcelled isle: year upon year, awaiting the return of my knights-fosterling. . . ."

Her voice grew weary.

"Foxkith's knighthood was the end of all. Youngest, bravest: the very last ever I managed to change back into a man. I can do no more. My power, too, is spent."

Russet Hannah stared at her. "But your foe is vanquished, his magic drained. . . ."

The Ancient Mother shook her head. "But not restored to me. Don't you see? It's the wand—can only be the wand. Only its return can heal my weakness." Hannah felt herself near panic as the other pursed her lips, made a dismissive little puff of breath. "That hoard he keeps? Mere gold: perfectly ordinary. Not a whiff of magic to it."

"But I must have Foxkith a man again!" Hannah cried.

"Soft, child," the wounded goddess soothed. Her fragile old limbs groaned as though ready to crack under their own weight. "Why do you ask *me* to restore him?"

"Because you're my one hope," the wayfarer girl exclaimed. "My sole recourse. If he's to be healed—"

"Hannah," whispered the tree. "Don't you know?"

"Know?" the henna-clad girl cried bitterly. Downy seeds floated from her hair. Lacy maplewings fluttered. An acorn dropped, followed by a hazelnut. Lost in her own despair, Hannah paid no attention. "What am I to know?" she asked. "I've dwelt my whole life in a twisted wood ruled by a wizard who told me nothing!"

The treewoman's tone grew conciliatory, her sad eyes concerned. "You say he never told you of his past, of his childhood here, his years abroad, this wound he dealt?"

The girl shook her head. Almonds and dates clattered softly. Eyeing the other's breast, she saw streaming sap had begun once more to flow as the rising sun warmed the night-cooled air. The goddess sighed.

"Restore Foxkith? Nothing could please me more. If I were healed . . ."

"Perhaps I could heal you," Hannah exclaimed suddenly, astonished that she had not thought of it before. "I've been a healer all my days. If I could—"

But the other barely shook her head, a faint smile still ghosting her lips. "No, my child. No doubt your gift is very great—I sense it—but my wound runs so woefully deep I doubt even your sweet healing can speedily restore me. For that I must rest years."

Hannah felt desperation seize her, her thoughts growing wild. She had not come all this way to be daunted now. Surely some word, some deed, some means must exist whereby the Ancient Mother might be persuaded to work the feat she so doggedly deemed impossible. The russet-garbed girl drew breath, poised to proffer some new plan or plea—she knew not what—but the other's calm, penetrating gaze halted her before she spoke.

"Why do you ask *me* to heal him, my dear?" the tree-woman repeated. "Your own powers, however unschooled, are so much greater than mine."

The outland girl stopped short, speechless, startled.

What could the other mean? Near the end of her strength, it seemed, the ancient deity heaved a painful sigh.

"You truly do not know? He gave you no inkling, then. That was his game: to keep the knowledge from you, and you from any close human contact, the cottars all afraid to speak—in hopes that you would never discover it, never puzzle it out."

"What are you saying?" Hannah managed. Lost in her own thoughts, the other seemed not to hear.

"Oh, he was false, false to the bone! How foolish my matron's bosom to have trusted and shielded, loved and excused him over and over again. Then he betrayed me the final time, and cut out my heart. So many years followed: him powerful beyond compare, I desperately enfeebled. Yet it must be righted somehow. So much I knew. For the world's sake."

Maddened, Hannah shifted from foot to foot. "Speak plainly," she begged, but the other only rambled.

"Few enough I was able to change, over the centuries: all the King's sons. Their cousins as well. When time came, I called them. They always gathered without complaint, my young courtiers putting themselves forward eagerly— though they scarcely understood the half of what I must ask them to do. All willing to hazard any danger for my sake."

Sadly, the Ancient Mother shook her head. Hannah clenched her teeth. In another moment, she felt she might scream. The other murmured as though dazed, falling into a doze, oblivious.

"All my knights-fosterling, these endless, seasonless years—waiting and waiting on their return. Surely one—if but one could return triumphant from that wizardly thief . . ."

"Who, as the Golden Boar, slew all of them save Foxkith!" Hannah could not keep the anguish from her words. "Could you contrive no means to risk lives other than those of innocents?"

Only this last seemed to penetrate the other's revery. The Ancient Mother roused herself, looked at the fair-haired girl.

"Seek him myself, you mean, leaving to starve all those left behind on my enchanted isle?"

The treewoman's voice was like distant flutes and reeds. Strangely, it held only amusement, no trace of reproach. The copper-garbed girl glanced uneasily at the thin, watchful creatures all around. Draggled jays in the treetop, mangy ground squirrels about the roots. Not far removed, a skinny mare suckled a spindle-legged foal. Wind sighed through the hair of the Sorcerer Queen.

"Even if I possessed the strength," the ancient one told Hannah gently, "after so many millennia, my roots are too deep. I doubt I could shift myself now without tearing apart the world."

Her tone grew pensive again.

"I sent forth no reluctant knights. All who embarked re-joiced at the chance. . . ."

Where was all this leading? Impatiently the girl before her exclaimed, "To challenge the Wizard and claim his hoard?"

"To find and recover my child, Hannah."

The russet girl fell abruptly silent. She felt as though the wind had been knocked from her ribs. She stood gaping, scarcely comprehending, struggling for breath.

"That pithy shoot the Wizard stole was my child," the ancient queen continued gently. "My own unborn self, taproot of my power, the very essence of the world's sorcery— of all magic, both mine and his."

She paused a moment, letting it sink in. Hannah could only stare at the other's visage. The ruts in the bark of that timeless face cut deep. Why had she never before this moment seen how closely it resembled her own? The other smiled.

"It's you. Don't you see, daughter? You are the prize he so strove to conceal: both captive maid and fabulous beast; the wand; the fabled, miraculous tree. Not gold or jewels, polished arms or silver cups. Hannah, *you* are the treasure at the heart of the Tanglewood."

Chapter 23
Treasure at the Heart of the Tanglewood

Hannah stood motionless, silent, transfixed. Breeze sighed and whispered about her. The Ancient Mother's words startled, stunned her—and yet, somewhere deep in her inmost being, she knew them to be true. The sorcerous air seemed to stir between them, silently resonating, almost shimmering. The russet-clad girl breathed deep.

"I am yours, then?" she murmured. The other nodded. Suddenly awkward, the fair girl shook herself. "But you're all of wood!" she protested. "Roots, bole, branches, leaves . . ."

"And what are you, my dear?" her mother asked. "Are you, too, not sprung from the same green growing stuff as I: fruits, flowers, leaves? Ah, in the spring, how glorious must be your flowers! Once, in my youth, I flowered so—and would flower again, could I but heal."

Russet Hannah scarcely heard. "The Wizard told me I

was his: his servant, his . . . conjurling." She put one hand to her brow, mazed at the thought. Little persimmons and pistachio nuts jostled coolly against her skin. "Oftentimes, I think, without his ever saying it, he half-wanted me to believe I was his child." Hannah set her teeth. "Well, I was *never* his child."

Before her, the Ancient Mother laughed wryly. "And yet, perhaps, in a way, you are. Had you remained sheltered in my breast, doubtless you'd have become more like me. Perhaps in time, we'd have grown into a great double-trunked tree, each bole mirroring the other, our hearts and minds and powers forever conjoined."

"But we were severed," Hannah whispered. Her seed-filled hair rustled, thistledown blowing, hawthorns dropping to the ground. "And grew apart."

Again the other nodded, sighing in a way that sounded only half nostalgic. Astonishment, perhaps even pleasure, made up the rest. "Part of you is a Wizard's child, though his servant no more. That never again."

"I grew up wanting to believe myself human," the woodland girl murmured, in some distress. Her mother managed a laugh.

"You're far more human than ever I guessed. I thought you'd be a tree, like me. Though I gadded about like a dandelion seed in my very youth, long before I reached your age, I'd taken root. How odd to see a child of mine sport legs!" The Ancient Mother laughed again, painfully feeble but genuinely amused at herself. "I thought my knights would find a fabulous sapling richly in flower, hid fast at the heart of the Tanglewood."

Russet Hannah gazed at the woodland queen, her age-old roots, rutted and swirling trunk, and innumerable limbs reaching into the sunwashed air. She saw now that the green sap bleeding from that sundered breast was the color of the tea she, Hannah, once had brewed for the Wizard: the draught he had drunk so greedily. It was the same which had bled from her own scalp the time he had pulled all her nascent shoots. Seeing, remembering this, Hannah found herself shivering.

"Truly," she breathed, "I am sprung from you."

Again the other nodded. "Flush with all the sap and vigor that ever I harbored in my most verdant youth."

Hannah stared at the silvery bole of the great tree, laced to the ground by innumerable runners, knobby and thick as human limbs. The runaway girl turned her gaze to her own smooth, white feet—which had brought her so far—just visible beneath the deep, pure russet of her gown.

"Will I become like you?" she asked. "Must I one day give up my travels and take root as you have done?"

Almost imperceptibly, the other shrugged. "Who can say?" she answered gently. "I took root because I felt the urge strong in my blood. You, too, may feel that urge in time—or not. It hardly matters. For what it's worth, I doubt any such stirrings will come to you for a very long time."

The two of them fell silent. Hannah listened to wind rustling the great tree's branches, to the green blood beating within her own veins.

"You say that I have powers," she ventured at last, "all that you yourself once wielded, before your wounding and the stealing away of . . . of me."

Lazily, her eyes half closed, almost as though she were falling asleep in the warm sunlight, the Ancient Mother assented.

"What powers are those?" Hannah asked her gravely.

Just barely, the treewoman yawned. "Telling everything of which you're capable would take such a long time, my dear. I'm weary from my ordeal. I've no doubt you'll discover all in time. How could you not? Magical knowledge is in your very blood."

"But what am I to do with it?" Hannah asked her. "To what use am I to put my powers?"

"Heal the world," murmured the ancient queen. "Indeed, you've already begun the task, whether or not you so intended—for numen flows and breathes and showers from you even as it used to do from me, and shall again, when I am healed."

Her great trunk groaned deeply, as though hardly able to bear the weight of so many limbs. Her eyes slipped shut, fluttered, opened again. Hannah moved closer.

"No, Mother," she pleaded. "Don't sleep. I need you."

The other smiled. "But I must sleep, child, a long, restorative slumber. How I wish I might remain awake and tell you all, but my strength's near run dry."

"But I've only just found you!" her daughter protested.

Once more the other slowly blinked. She whispered, "Simply remember that you're sprung from me. My wisdom's in you. So, too, my folly. Look to your inmost heart to find all you need to restore the world. Beware of flatterers."

Hannah gazed at her ancient face, shaped in the smooth furrows of the silvery bark as though carved there: her own face gazing out at her, her own voice speaking in the rustle of the leaves.

"Daughter, you are me, and I you. We're the same substance, the same being—though I am now the Ancient Mother and you my Maidenly incarnation." Mischievously, she glanced at Foxkith. "Though about to become the Matron, I think."

Again the treewoman yawned, more broadly this time, no longer able to keep sleep at bay. "Child, I tire. Now that you're returned to me and the world, I must rest."

Her eyes strayed shut a final time. Calm within herself at last, for the first time since she had beheld the tree, Hannah understood what she must do. Gently, she laid her palms on either side of the great rift cleaving the ancient's wooden breast. The scarred halves were old, weathered, their edges dulled and polished by time. Yet sap still flowed slick and sluggish from the heart-deep wound. Warmth infused the hands of the fair-haired girl, power beating through her blood, rising within her like sap from the center of the tree.

The scent of sorcery filled the air. Beneath Hannah's touch, the wood softened, becoming malleable. She found herself bending the gashed sides of the chasm inward, pressing them toward one another. They fused effortlessly, first the inmost layers of dense heartwood, then the sapwood without. Finally the rutted bark joined together, leaving no seam. As the green and bleeding flow halted, she heard the Ancient Mother sigh.

"Rest," Hannah urged her, "and when at last you rouse, the world will be a different place. Sleep, while I prepare for your awakening."

Hannah kissed the other's cheek, so hard and smooth, and yet so strangely like her own. The forest queen stood, eyes closed, her breathing even, face turned a little to one side. It looked serene, the woodland girl realized, free of pain for the first time, finally at rest. Hannah watched a perfect leaf-bud sprout upon the gray wood of the Ancient Mother's cheek. Her branches stirred. As she watched, the russet-clad girl beheld elsewhere other leaves, still small, forming, beginning to unfurl.

Hannah glanced around her. Pineseed and thistledown streamed from her hair, spinning away across the rocky expanse that surrounded the slumbering tree. Barren no more, she saw—and strangely, felt no surprise. All was becoming as it should be. The former waste lay covered now with sedge and winter rye. Young oaks with sienna foliage, sweet-gum saplings with flaming leaves dotted the soil. Pyrocantha and bittersweet clambered over the rocks. A holly bush nodded amid the rest. She found herself laughing with delight.

Badger lay snoring softly at her feet. Hannah knelt and kissed one shaggy paw. With a snort and a chuff, he turned over and, in the next instant, became a sleeping man. Old and bearded with wispy salt-and-pepper hair, he slept on, oblivious. Very thick about the middle and not much taller than Hannah, he lay clad in a jerkin striped black, white, and gray. A green embroidery of leaves trimmed his collar, hem, and cuffs. Never opening his eyes, he scratched absently behind one ear with a thick, callused hand, and settled back into snores.

"Fancy it!" Magpie exclaimed, fluttering down from her perch upon the Ancient Mother to occupy the shoulder of the harvest-haired girl. The bird stared at the slumbering man. "Looks like Broc, the gardener."

"I could have restored you all long since," Hannah murmured, by turns awed and incensed, "if I'd but known!"

"Well, you didn't," Magpie chattered. "It's the learning of *that* that's taken you all this time, not the knowing how."

Hannah turned to the black-and-white bird and blew across the down on the other's breast. With a shriek, Magpie catapulted to the ground and lay there flipping among the new-sprung grass. A moment later, she was a floundering woman of middle years, big-boned, rather angular and tall, in a long gray and black shift with a white baker's apron. Black satin ribbons formed the apron strings, which trailed long behind her.

"A little warning!" she squawked, picking herself up from the ground and beating off the dust. "I wasn't expecting that."

"Who were you?" Hannah asked.

"Magret," the other answered, flapping her arms. "The King's cook. The Wizard brought a handful of us along to rear you and save himself the trouble." She shook her long, slender fingers out and stared at them. "I'd gotten used to the wings."

Hannah's gaze fell on the red foxlets poised furtive at the edge of the great tree's shade—watchfully silent for once.

"*They* won't want to be made human again," the cook muttered, smoothing back her hair, which was dark with streaks of iron gray and one white lock, pulled into a bun at the nape of her neck. "They've relished every ounce of mischief they've made while in their foxy shape."

"Who are they?" Hannah inquired.

"My nephews: Rust, Red, and Merry, the royal ostler's children. I looked after them in the kitchen during the day. My ginger-pated knave of a brother will answer for their wanton ways, you can be sure. I'll have to find him first."

"All will be found," Hannah laughed, "and all restored. But why did you never tell me this before?"

"It only just came back to me!" the raw-boned woman exclaimed. "When I saw the Ancient Matriarch and her wound. Broc remembered too, then, I'm sure. I can't say about our red-haired scamps. They're scarcely more than babes."

Hannah turned. "Magpie," she said softly, "what am I?"

The tall woman blinked. "Well, the child of the Ancient Mother, of course. Haven't you ears?"

Hannah suppressed a smile. "And the Mother herself?"

"She makes things grow—your task now."

The cook gazed at the many creatures—grouse and marsh hens, marmots and voles—once more browsing eagerly all around, but of the bounty of the manna-haired girl now, not the ancient queen. Some of them glanced at Hannah from time to time, but most seemed too busy to pay her any heed. Their air of desperation had entirely evaporated, replaced by one of relief, contentment, even industry. Nodding, the cook continued frankly.

"Restore them. They'll tell you. Poke that lazy Broc awake. He knows all about shoots and slips and scions and grafts. Don't ask me. I tend hearth."

Hannah cast her gaze about the clearing, knee-high now in mare's tails and thistle. The little trees were branching out. Deer grazed. Mice gorged on cloudberries burdening slender bushes that had not been there the hour before. Pips and seeds continued to tumble from her hair. Birch seedlets spun away on the air. Fat currants fell. Walnuts and almonds dropped. Dried pods burst, spilled rolling peas of russet, yellow, and green upon the ground. Eagerly the animals feasted. The fair-haired girl fingered her locks.

"I keep changing."

The King's cook snorted, running it off like a litany: "Winter Damsel, Spring Maid, Summer Girl, and Autumn Lass—four seasons are a sight better than the Wizard's drab eternal cold."

Hannah felt a little dizzied. "He told me my leaving would kill him—and me."

"Nonsense!" the other laughed. "Still kicking, isn't he? You, too. And won't he be the lively snit when you and Foxkith return to the Tanglewood to seize his gold and return it to all those to whom it rightfully belongs?"

The Autumn Lass nodded, sobered, added, "After I've set this isle to rights."

The woman with the gray-barred hair eyed her. "Don't let it wait too long," she answered tartly. "That sneakthief fairly cries out to be served up fit and finally."

A rolling roar of distant thunder—or perhaps it was only waves surging unseen against the strand far, far below. Again Russet Hannah nodded.

"Indeed," she pledged. "I'll call him to account. The Ancient Mother said he must pay the price, and so he shall."

She thought a long moment, dark and deep, then resolved herself. No matter how she might loathe the necessity, a reckoning there must be.

"It wasn't just the lives of knights he took," Hannah said at last, "but those of countless cottars, too. He deserves to be cast into beast-shape for all eternity—and not that of a magical boar. A mere mortal one, set at liberty within the greenwood—that all he's wronged may hunt him there, if so they choose."

"Just so." The tall woman in the apron nodded approvingly. "May he never know a moment's peace." Dusting off her hand, she added, "I fancy a nice round of suckling pork for dinner, myself."

Despite herself, the girl could not suppress a smile. Foxkith sprang up, voiceless, panting. He watched her intently, expectantly. Kneeling, she gathered him into her arms.

"Foxkith," she asked, "King's son and now King of this isle, have you known me all the while—or only from time to time?" He licked her cheek, tickling. "In your heart, perhaps," she chuckled, "if not always in mind. Do you ken my words now? Did you know all along I could restore both your manhood and your voice at one stroke?"

A snort from the shadow fox then that sounded like laughter. Ever so gently, he nipped her cheek. Hannah smiled, feeling giddy. So much, still, to discover of this island and the world. When next the Ancient Mother woke, they must speak again, though how long the great tree that had given her life would remain dormant, healing, she could not guess. Work enough in plenty to occupy her until then. Wind fanned her burning amber gown. Her plenteous hair lifted, beat, raining, wondrously bountiful. Foxkith turned, struggled, eager in her arms. Laughing, she bent to kiss the milk-white lily on his breast.